The Ghost Walked Across the Floor Toward Cinnamon.

"Will you help me find Emily?" Felix asked. "You can help. You can talk and ask people. I think they took her away. Alive and dead they took her from me."

His hands were touching me, ghost hands. The ghost eyes, filled with misery, looked into mine. "Please help me. I have to find her. You'll never see me again."

"Let go of me," I whispered fiercely, but he didn't and I knew what was going to happen.

"Emily liked to dance," he said, and the ghost hands were strong, pulling me toward him, moving me so that I had to move too or be dragged. And then we were dancing in some unreal nightmare dance across the floor.

GHOST BEHIND ME

EVE BUNTING

AN ARCHWAY PAPERBACK
Published by POCKET BOOKS
New York   London   Toronto   Sydney   Tokyo

AN ARCHWAY PAPERBACK *Original*

An Archway Paperback published by
POCKET BOOKS, a division of Simon & Schuster Inc.
1230 Avenue of the Americas, New York, NY 10020

ISBN: 0-671-62211-0

First Archway Paperback printing March 1984

10 9 8 7 6 5

AN ARCHWAY PAPERBACK and colophon are
registered trademarks of Simon & Schuster Inc.

Printed in the U.S.A.

IL 7+

Chapter 1

The ghost came to call on the first night we moved into the new house—though of course I didn't know then that he was a ghost, or that I'd become so involved with him.

The house was new to us but very old. It stood on a street called Anderson Street that rose up from San Francisco Bay like a roller coaster with three dips. The house hung over the edge of the top dip, as if about to plunge on some mad ride into the water below. It was made of overlapping wood shingles, like lizard skin, and whoever had built it all those years ago had put in jillions of windows of all shapes and sizes. There was even an arched one, and one small and round, like the porthole in a ship.

My little brother, JoJo, kept running about before we were even unpacked.

"It's huge, Dad. All these bedrooms. But how come there's only one bath? You'd better tell Cinnamon not to stay in there for hours and hours. We'll never get a turn."

Dad smiled. "Cinnamon's not all that bad. When you're sixteen, you'll want to spend as much time in the bathroom as she does."

"Besides," I said, "what you don't understand, JoJo, is that some people like to *wash*."

"Faddle!" JoJo said. *Faddle* is his favorite word for this week. I wish he'd stopped with that. But then he said, "Gee, even if Mom and Marissa were here, there'd still be loads of room." I could tell he knew he shouldn't have said it the second the words were out. But at seven it's hard to remember what not to say. Dad got that tight, hurting look on his face and I felt the misery welling up inside me. It's a funny thing about misery. It's always there. But sometimes the level goes down, like water in a reservoir. Then something is said or remembered, and it fills up again, ready to overflow.

Dad ruffled JoJo's hair. "Well, it's just us three. So everyone gets to choose a room. Of course, I'm already installed."

Dad had stayed in the house for three nights before he flew up to Boston and drove us back. He had rented the place furnished for the next three months from people called the Rookwoods who were artists and who had gone to Europe for the summer. By the time they got back we would have found a house of our own and brought our furniture from storage. Dad is an engineer and he has been transferred here to work on BART, which is short for Bay Area Transit System. The house is in Sausalito, a little town across the bridge from the city, so it's pretty convenient.

2

"What do you think, Cinnamon?" he'd asked me when the transfer came through. "Maybe it would be good. For JoJo. For all of us."

I knew he wanted to go, not only to get away, but because of the job. You can hide behind a job. You can work longer hours. It helps cover up the pain. I guess Dad always was a kind of workaholic. I remember the way Mom used to tease him. These days, he's fully involved in his work.

I saw him looking at his watch now, and I knew he wanted to get in his car and leave for the office.

"Go, Dad," I said. "JoJo and I can unpack without you."

"You're sure you don't mind? I'll be home about six."

"I don't mind."

I walked down the stairs with him, and we picked our way through the cartons we'd dragged inside and left in the hallway. Familiar things poked out of the loosely tied boxes. Two of the wheels of JoJo's skateboard. The bruised pink satin toe of one of my ballet slippers. I looked away. Why had we brought that?

The house has a semicircular driveway at the side so you can go in one space in the wall that edges the street and out the other. There's no way the entrance could be at the front because there's nothing there except a tangled crop of weeds and grass. Here, from the door, I could watch Dad's car go down the roller coaster street, where fog filled the hollows, and disappear in the thicker fog that hid the highway by the edge of the bay.

I looked around. This damp, gray fog wasn't what I'd expected from California. It hung in tatters from

3

the trees and trailed its fingers through the heavy air. For a minute I felt as if I couldn't breathe, and I shivered and hurried back inside.

"Bring me some Fig Newtons if you're coming upstairs," JoJo yelled. "Bring the package, okay?"

Once I'd have said, "Get them yourself." But mostly now I go overboard for JoJo. Face it, he and Dad are all the family I have left, except for Aunt Clara who lives in Rome. And I try not to think about her or Rome, because of what happened. Also I guess I'm extra nice to JoJo because I'm trying to make up to him all the time for Mom and Marissa. Not that their dying was my fault. Mrs. Abbot, my shrink, has been over that with me at least a jillion times. And I believe her. Sort of. Anyway, I went in the kitchen now for the Fig Newtons and took them upstairs.

I found JoJo lying on the mattress on the bed of the porthole room, which he'd already tagged. He was reading the Space War comic Dad had bought him on our last freeway stop. I threw him the cookies and went to inspect the other three bedrooms that were still available.

One was real square and ordinary. It didn't even seem to belong in this old, crooked house. One had a sloping ceiling and windows that pushed out on metal bars. If Marissa had been here, we'd have fought over this one. Oh, Marissa! Gently, I closed the door. That left the fourth room, which wasn't a bedroom at all. The Rookwoods had stored a bunch of junk in it—old, peeling canvases, squeezed-out tubes of paint, stuck-together brushes. I saw two trunks, old-fashioned ones with metal bands around them. Books were piled on

4

the floor. This was the room with the tall, arched window, the kind you might see in a cathedral. But there was no glass in it. I leaned out. Below was the curve of driveway and the street beyond. Fog drifted around my head, wafting like smoke. Through its blur I saw a house across from us, half hidden by trees. I turned back and studied the room. The wallpaper was faded pink with roses arched across it. The floor was bare, wooden and very dirty. I tried to imagine it swept and polished. There was a perfume that seemed to come and go as if carried on the wisps of fog.

It was a nice room, and Dad would probably let me get glass in that empty window. I sat yogi fashion on the dirty floor. I liked it.

"You're taking this one?" JoJo stood in the doorway.

"Yep." I jumped up and began gathering up books right away. "Help me get this stuff out, will you, JoJo? I'll put everything in Marissa's room. . . ." I stopped. "I mean, in the room with the sloping roof. And I'll bring that furniture in here."

"But why? You'll have to clean everything. And the other room's prettier. If Marissa was here, she'd . . ." JoJo stopped. "Oh, I'll help you, Cinnamon-Pie." For a little punk kid who's obnoxious a lot of the time JoJo can be pretty tuned in. "Did you know there's no glass in the window?" he asked.

"I know."

"Aren't you afraid of . . . something . . . coming in?"

Coldness touched my neck. "What do you mean, something?"

JoJo shrugged. "I dunno. A cat, maybe." But I

5

knew he hadn't meant a cat. The trouble with JoJo is that he reads too many comics. "Somebody, then," he went on. "A bad guy."

"He'd have to be Spiderman," I said. "There's no tree outside."

"Drainpipe," JoJo said. "Ivy."

"Nothing," I told him. "All that's coming in that window is fog."

"Could be something that flies," JoJo said. "A vampire."

"Stop it," I shrieked. "Now you are really scaring me."

JoJo smiled.

I wasn't truly scared. But I decided I would ask Dad right away for glass in that window space.

JoJo helped me move the first trunk. Every time we stopped to rest he flapped his arms like vampire wings and bared his fangs. I pretended not to see.

By five we had the room emptied, except for the dusty pictures on the walls. These weren't Rookwood pictures, which were all over the rest of the house, big blobs of color in bright blues and reds. These were old-fashioned prints. When I wiped the dust off one, I saw a little girl dressed in her mother's clothes winking at herself in a mirror. HE'LL LOVE ME IN THIS, the caption said. The other one had a boy wearing his father's giant boots. Below, it said, IN DAD'S FOOT-STEPS.

"Yuk," I muttered. "Talk about sexist! And talk about a couple of dopey-looking kids." I pulled one down, leaving a colorless square on the wallpaper behind. Something fluttered to lie at my feet.

I picked it up, suddenly aware again of the heavy

6

scent of roses. It was a postcard, hand-painted and hand-lettered. On the front was drawn a dark red rose, so vivid and perfect that it could have been real. I turned it over. On the back was printed, TO MY DARK AND LOVELY VALENTINE. There was no signature, no postmark. It had been personally delivered. I stood, holding it, feeling weak and dizzy. The rose seemed to be growing larger, coming off the card to float in front of my eyes. I shook my head, blinked and focused on the picture that had hidden the card. The back was covered with brown paper, brittle now. The tape that stuck the edges to the wooden frame had peeled away at the bottom and the card had dropped from behind. I stripped the paper away. There was nothing else there.

To my dark and lovely valentine. Who was she? Who was he? The perfume wafted around me, too strong, too powerful.

JoJo had come back in.

"Are we going to make up the beds or not? I thought you wanted me to help you. It's okay if you don't."

"JoJo?" My voice had almost deserted me. "JoJo, do you smell roses?"

JoJo wrinkled his nose and gave a giant sniff. "Roses? Are you bonkers? All I smell is dust and spider's fur. And bugs' breath. Did you know that bug breath is really terrible? It's a scientific fact."

"Oh, JoJo," I said. "Let's just make up the beds." From the door I looked back at the empty room, not expecting to see anything, seeing nothing.

We got the Rookwood sheets from the linen closet. I decided I'd sleep in the square room tonight so I could clean in my room some more tomorrow.

"Yuk," JoJo said. "Who ever heard of black sheets?"

"They're probably very artistic," I told him.

JoJo looked suddenly cheerful. "Hey! They probably don't show dirt!"

I was only half listening. My dark and lovely valentine. Whoever he was, he must have loved her very much. And whoever he was, he wasn't a Rookwood, that I knew. The rose did not have the Rookwood touch. I shoved JoJo off to take a shower and went back in my new, empty room to look again at the card. I was still holding it when I heard Dad's car coming up the hill and turning into the driveway.

"Dad's home," I called. I'd show him the card and ask him if he could smell roses. Of course he'd be able to. JoJo had pretended he couldn't, just to scare me. But would even JoJo do that to me now, after all that had happened? He might. Anyway, Dad was home. I couldn't see his car, but I could hear it right beneath me. The fog moved around below, parting and coming together again, dividing to let me see the whole curve of the driveway. No car. But I could still hear it. Now wait just a second! Where was it? I leaned as far as I dared and then I realized that there must be a carport below, one that I hadn't noticed. But why wasn't Dad turning off the engine?

"JoJo," I called again. "Dad's here. Come on."

I put the postcard on top of the picture on the floor and raced down the stairs. Jumping the scatter of boxes in the hall, I pulled open the door.

Immediately the fog rushed in, as though it had knocked, and I'd answered.

I pushed through it and outside. There was no car. It

must be on the street then, though it sounded closer. I ran to the gap in the wall and looked. There was nothing on the street but gray waves of fog, rolling up endlessly from the bay below.

I started back, then stopped and stared. Something was falling in small plops, falling from nowhere, right there, right in front of me, like big drops of dark rain, falling in one place to make a spreading, black stain, thick like tar, thick like blood. And there was the engine sound, too, revving up now, drowning out the terrified thumping of my heart.

"JoJo," I called weakly, and I edged around in a wide safe circle and backed to the open door of the old house. Then I turned and slammed it closed behind me.

Chapter 2

I leaned against the door, every bit of me straining to hear the motor of the invisible car outside.

JoJo was pounding down the stairs. "Where's Dad? Wait for me!"

"Shh," I said.

The roar of the engine filled the room, vibrating off the white walls, rushing up the stairs to pulse itself out again through the windowless window. The house seemed filled with fog. I closed my eyes.

And then the motor revved even louder . . . putt . . . putt . . . putt, and roared away, dwindling to silence.

I opened my eyes cautiously.

The fog had gone. There was just the house now: the plain, wooden furniture, the Rookwood pictures splashing from the white walls. And JoJo on the stairs.

"Are you okay, Cinnamon?" His voice was shaky. "You look as if you're going to throw up."

"Didn't you hear anything there? Don't give me a

hard time, JoJo. Tell me honestly. Didn't you hear a car?"

"Uh-uh." His eyes were wide and scared. Not because he'd heard a ghost car, but because I looked weird to him, and he'd seen me look weird before. He took another step down the stairs.

"Is Dad here?" Small voice. Skinny little neck pulled down into his T-shirt.

I made myself move from the door. "No. I thought I heard him. But it was . . . somebody else." I tried to make my words normal. "What took you so long, anyway?"

JoJo gave a sigh. I could tell he was glad that big sister was back to being her own rotten self again.

"I had to brush my teeth." He pulled his lips back with his fingers in a horrible leer. "You always tell me to brush after Fig Newtons."

"Okay, JoJo," I said. "You stay here. I'm going outside for a second."

I opened the door the smallest crack, peering around it. There was nothing in the driveway but the changing layers of fog, shifting and moving, lying in wait beneath the wall that paralleled the street.

I found the switch that put on the porch light, though it wasn't dark yet. The yellow gleam shimmered, turning red at its edges.

I stepped outside and went slowly down the three wooden steps to the driveway, walking toward the shining, black stain. I walked carefully, my arms stretched shoulder high in front to guard me from a bump into invisible objects, to give me an early warning to run. I was like a little kid in third grade, looking for the donkey to pin the tail on. My arms moved up and down, finding nothing. I stopped at the wet splotch, crouched and touched it with my finger. Greasy. Slimy. I knew it was motor oil. I straightened, holding up my finger to the slanting yellow light from the porch.

I almost jumped from my body when two voices spoke at once, one in front of me, one behind.

The one behind I recognized. "Cinnamon?" JoJo croaked.

The other voice was coming from the wall and I peered through the fog and saw something balanced on top . . . a head . . . a head, just sitting there like a forgotten beach ball.

I backed up three steps and bumped into JoJo. Of course it wasn't a head! What was the matter with me? It was someone peering over from the other side. I saw shoulders and a chest now, a full person, a guy vaulting over into our driveway.

He loped across where the invisible car had been, plonking one foot right in the oil drip. I saw no black footprint as he strode toward us.

"I hope I didn't frighten you," he said.

I took a deep breath. "Of course not. Why would I be frightened? I just thought a cut-off head was talking to me out of the fog. There's nothing frightening in that."

He grinned. "Sorry."

"You could have come through the gate, you know. There was no need to climb over."

His grin widened. "That's what Alison used to say. She lived in the Rookwood house last summer. Like I told her, I never do things the easy way."

"Who are you?" JoJo asked. There's one thing about having a little brother around. You don't have to mess around finding out stuff. He does it for you.

"I'm Paul Russell. I live just across the street."

"I'm John Joseph Cameron but everybody calls me JoJo. She's Cinnamon."

"Cinnamon? I've heard of cinnamon rolls and cinnamon toast but never a cinnamon person."

"I know about the rolls and the toast," I said coldly. "I've heard all of that stuff before. Usually from JoJo."

"She's called that for our grandmother who was from New Orleans," JoJo told him. "She's not alive anymore."

Did Paul notice the quick look JoJo give me? Not alive any more. Neither were Mom and Marissa. But Grandma had been old, old. And she'd died in her own bed, in her own old house. They . . .

"I was on my way home from work and I saw you come out of the house," Paul said. "At first I thought you were sleepwalking. Honest. That's why I stopped and looked over. I don't usually stare into strange yards. Of course, most people don't sleepwalk with all their clothes on. But I figured maybe you were napwalking . . . ? Then you began poking at the ground."

I looked at the shiny blob on my finger. "I was looking at this. What do you think it is?"

JoJo and Paul both craned forward.

"Your finger?" JoJo asked.

"It *looks* like a finger," Paul said. "But I couldn't be certain."

"I'm talking about the black stuff *on* my finger."

13

"What black stuff?"

I knew it was dark, but it wasn't that dark. "This black stuff." I wiped the gook off on the front of Paul's pale blue nylon windbreaker, leaving a slimy black trail, like a snail track.

"Ooops," I said, "I shouldn't have done that. Look, I'm sorry. I'll wash your jacket or have it cleaned for you."

Paul was looking down at his front, and I could tell he was puzzled. "You're sorry about what?"

I put my hand across my mouth. I couldn't believe it. It was there, and he couldn't see it.

"Cinnamon?" JoJo's voice was nervous. "Are you okay, Cinnamon-Pie? Maybe you do need to throw up."

"Have you been sick?" Paul asked.

I swallowed. "No, no." But I wasn't sure any more. "Could you come here a sec, both of you."

They followed me back to the oil leak. I pointed down. "Would you do me a favor. Would you touch that?"

"You mean the driveway?"

I nodded. "Right there."

Paul crouched and JoJo crouched beside him. "Cinnamon . . ." JoJo began.

"It's all right, JoJo," I said. "We'll go in the house in just a minute. Touch the driveway for me, okay?"

Paul put his hand flat, the edge of it brushing the oil pool. JoJo's went right in it.

"It's cold," Paul said. I could tell he didn't know what I wanted from him. "Is this some sort of game?" I didn't answer him.

"JoJo?"

14

"It's not *that* cold." He moved his hand in circles. JoJo didn't know what I wanted either. They both stood up, and I looked at their hands. Clean. My heart had begun to race like one of Dad's trains rattling along the track.

And then I heard a car engine, and the train inside me stopped and started again with a jerk. "Oh, no," I whispered. Headlights came dazzling through the fog, turning in at our gate.

"It's Dad," JoJo said, and I sensed his relief. Dad was home and *he* could cope with spaced-out old Cinnamon-Stick.

The three of us moved back to the porch, and Dad drove in and stopped in front. He turned off lights and motor and opened the door.

JoJo sniffed. "I think I smell pizza."

"Right." Dad was leaning into the back seat, lugging out a big, square box. "Sausage and mushroom."

JoJo ran to him, and I stood with Paul. The porch light shone on Paul's hair, black as my own, but straight and fairly short, where mine was long and curly. His eyes were dark, too, under dark brows. I guessed he was probably seventeen. I guessed too that if this had been an ordinary night I'd have been real jazzed to meet a cute guy like this straight off. I'd have been writing to Jenny, my best friend back in Boston, and telling her how awesome he was. But this wasn't an ordinary night. And I didn't have a friend called Jenny, or any friends anymore. And I didn't write letters to Boston.

JoJo was coming carefully up the steps, carrying the pizza box, and Dad was behind with his heavy brief-case.

"This is Paul," JoJo said. "He lives across the street. He came to see what was wrong with . . ." He stopped. "He saw Cinnamon."

Dad shook Paul's hand. "That's nice. Would you like to come in and share our pizza? I bought it in that pizza place at the bottom of the hill, so I don't know if it will be good."

Paul smiled. "It'll be real good. I work there. But I'll tell you the truth. If there's one thing I can't stand to eat anymore, it's pizza."

Dad smiled too. "That figures." He went in behind JoJo.

"I'd better go," Paul said to me. "Maybe I'll see you tomorrow."

I nodded, suddenly thinking of something, hoping. I touched his arm. "You were coming from work. You didn't drive into our driveway before you went over to your own house? You didn't leave your motor running and then . . ."

"Heck no. All I have today is a bicycle. It's fine flying down those hills in the morning, but coming home, man! There's no way I can make it all the way up Everest here. I ride to the first hump, get off and push."

"Oh." Of course there wasn't going to be any reasonable explanation.

Paul was looking down at me and I sensed something, a softness, a friendliness.

"Is there anything wrong? You seem upset. I didn't really scare you, did I?"

"No," I said. "It's just . . . the strange house and everything."

"Yeah." He stood back, looking up at the lizard-skin shingles, way, way up at the arched window. For a minute I thought he was going to say something, something important, but he only shrugged. "Well, see you, I hope."

I watched him go, standing under the light with one hand on the doorknob, ready to push the door open and jump inside if a shadow moved.

He vaulted the wall again. I guessed the bicycle was propped on the other side. In a second his arm came up in a wave. "Bye," he yelled.

I stood for a second, thinking. What a way to meet him! I could imagine him telling his friends or the guys in the pizza parlor about it. "There's a new girl just moved into the house across the street. She's not bad-looking, but wouldn't you know my luck? She's a total airhead."

The heck with it, I thought, and I went in and closed the door.

Sitting with Dad and JoJo in the Rookwood kitchen it all began to seem unreal. The rose that grew and grew and filled the room with perfume. The car that wasn't there. The oil that only I could see. I secretly lifted my finger and examined the stain on it, dry now, looking as though I'd dipped it in black dye.

Dad picked an anchovy from his slice of pizza and set it on his napkin. He topped up my glass with Dr. Pepper. "I'm sorry I was late tonight. That traffic on the Golden Gate bridge is unbelievable. Everything crawls." He took another slice of pizza. "How did the unpacking go?"

"Fine," I said.

"Me and her made the beds," JoJo told him. "But she's going to move into the room with no glass in the window."

"No, I'm not," I said quickly. "I changed my mind. I'm going to take the big square room."

"Good. Fine." Dad had finished eating, and I saw him glance surreptitiously at his briefcase. "I'll catch up on a little work this evening, and then I'll take an hour in the morning so we can all go to the market. Maybe you could make a list, Cinnamon."

"Put down Fig Newtons," JoJo ordered.

Everything seemed so normal now, even in this different house. Dad excused himself to go to the dining room and spread his papers on the table. There wasn't much washing up to do, and afterwards JoJo and I fought over the TV programs.

We went to bed before Dad did.

After I'd brushed my teeth, I went to tuck JoJo in. I'd taken that over since Mom died. He was half asleep already, his face turned to the wall. I saw that he had his thumb in his mouth.

"No, JoJo," I whispered. "Don't suck your thumb." He'd done this when he was a baby, I guess, but he'd stopped when he was about two. It had started for a while after Mom and Marissa had died and then stopped. Now he'd begun again.

He took the thumb out, and I tucked his arm under the sheet. "Cinnamon?" he asked sleepily. "You don't think Dad could be killed going across that bridge? You don't think another car could bash into him and make him fall way down into the water?"

"Definitely not," I said. "You heard him. They all crawl along. Go to sleep now, JoJo."

18

"Cinnamon?"

"Yes?"

"Are you okay?"

"Sure I'm okay."

"Promise?"

"Promise." I closed his door gently. Poor little old JoJo. If Dad got shoved off the bridge, and Cinnamon got taken away again to the hospital, who'd be left? People you loved could disappear on you awful fast.

I lay in the big square ordinary room that had an ordinary door and four ordinary windows, all closed against the night and the fog, and I wished we were all safely back in Massachusetts.

The house sounds were new to me and I lay listening. Probably in a wind, the house would creak, the wood shifting like the timbers of an old ship. Tonight everything was muffled. I heard the faraway moan of a foghorn in bay or ocean. A dog barked.

After a few minutes I switched on the lamp and got out of bed. The floor creaked as I walked across to my overnight bag. I'd brought it with me into all the motel rooms on the way here, and I knew exactly where to find what I was looking for . . . my mother's silver hairbrush.

The brush was part of a set that had a hand mirror and a comb. They were heavy, embossed silver with her initials—CA—for Celia Arnaud. Her parents had given them to her on her sixteenth birthday, and now they were mine.

I'd seen my mother, night after night, brushing her dark hair with this silver brush. Her eyes would meet mine in the mirror and she'd smile and I'd just stand there, watching her, comforted by the rise and fall of her arm, the gleam of the silver under the lamplight.

Tonight I carried the brush with me back to bed and slipped it under my pillow, my hand around the handle. JoJo had his thumb and I had this. Oh, Mama, if you were only here.

I heard Dad come upstairs. I heard him open JoJo's door and go in, and a few minutes later he came to me. I lay very still. One part of me wanted to tell him all the strange things that had happened today, to ask him to protect me, to beg him to take us back to Massachusetts. But another part knew I wouldn't. He'd think I was getting sick again. Maybe he'd call Dr. Abbot, and maybe they'd think I should go somewhere and let a bunch of psychiatrists tell me all over again how to handle stress and pain.

I kept my eyes closed, and I felt Dad's lips brush my forehead. I tried not to cry.

It was much, much later when I heard the car. Its roar filled the room, lifting me from the edge of sleep. It was calling, pulling at me.

I got out of bed.

There was only one room that overlooked the curve of the driveway where the car waited. I opened my door to the darkness that lay between the rooms and stood very still.

I heard JoJo cough, a small muffled sound, and I saw that the fog was there, drifting in a straight stream from the open door of the rose room.

My feet were cold.

I walked slowly, clutching the silver brush. And the strangeness was back. I was sleepwalking . . . not here . . . not anywhere.

The rose scent closed around me as I crossed the

room and kneeled at the windowless window.

I'd known there'd be only sound below. Only the motor churning. And then that, too, stopped.

An invisible door on the invisible car slammed.

I heard no footsteps, but I knew that someone now stood below the window, looking up at me.

Chapter 3

I don't know what broke the spell. I just knew suddenly that I was here, leaning out of this dark, empty window and that I had to get away from whatever watched me from below. I turned and half stumbled, half ran from the room.

After Mom and Marissa died, JoJo used to creep all the time into *my* bed at night. Tonight I was the one who crept into his. He didn't waken as I moved him over and lay rigidly beside him. The porthole window was a pale circle in the deep darkness. I could see the gleam of the mirror above the dresser and the bulk of the big, overstuffed chair that crouched in the corner.

My fingers tightened on the silver hairbrush in my hand.

"She's gone, Cinnamon. They're both gone," Susan Abbot, Susan Shrink had said. "Let them go, honey. It's right to remember and you'll always remember. But don't torture yourself like this."

22

Easy for her to say. In the end I'd learned how to act so that she'd think I was better.

"I *have* learned not to blame myself. Honest," I'd said.

Her eyes had always softened, though I'd never been a hundred percent sure she believed me. Shrinks are probably on the lookout for lies.

Death. Ghosts. I tried to make my mind a blank. The trick was to concentrate on a spot in the middle of your forehead. But the ghost kept creeping back in. Who was he? Had I really heard something, felt something or was I imagining it? That possibility was worse than the possibility of the ghost.

I turned restlessly in the bed and heard the suck, suck, sucking begin as JoJo found his thumb. Poor little JoJo. He wasn't finding it easy to let the bad memories go either.

If I *was* imagining something as real as the motor of that car, as real as the oil and the smell of roses, then maybe this time I had really and truly flipped. What was it they called it? Maybe I'd crossed the invisible line?

"Do you mean between being sane and being crazy?" I'd asked Susan Shrink.

She'd sounded shocked. "Of course not, Cinnamon." Then what *did* it mean? Nobody ever said.

The night was as long as ten nights. Daylight was brightening the porthole when I finally slept.

I wakened to JoJo jabbing at me.

Sunshine filled the room with its dazzle. JoJo was sitting up in the bed, staring down at me. Suddenly I remembered the terror of last night. But it didn't seem so terrifying now. I remembered my panic that I was going crazy. That seemed ridiculous too. Of course I wasn't crazy. It had been only a dream. Anyone could have a dream that seemed close enough to touch. I stretched.

"How come you're not wearing your PJ's, JoJo? You're not supposed to sleep in your underwear."

"How come you're in my bed?" JoJo asked indignantly.

"I must have sleepwalked."

"Well, go walk the other way next time," JoJo told me. "I'm too big to sleep with my sister."

I lifted the pillow and jammed it against his skinny little stomach. Mornings were so much better than nights. Sometimes I wished that night would never come.

I heard Dad down in the kitchen then, and I jumped out of bed. The brush had fallen from my hand while I slept, and I picked it up and rubbed it on my nightgown before I set it on JoJo's dresser. He pattered behind me, grabbing his jeans and T-shirt, touching the shine of the brush as he passed. For a second our eyes met in the mirror and slid away.

Sunlight danced in the corridor. Through the open door of the rose room I could see dust hanging in a dazzle in front of the empty arch of window. No rose smell, no fog, no phantom car. It had been a nightmare all right. Still, I hurried down the stairs.

"Good morning." Dad was eating cereal at the kitchen table. "There's only this and a couple of rolls for breakfast. As soon as you're ready we'll go to the market."

I nodded and sat opposite him.

24

Never had I eaten cereal so slowly. I pushed the spoon round and round in my almost empty dish. There was no way I wanted to rush back upstairs to get dressed.

Dad looked at his watch. "Hurry it up, sweetie. I have to get to work."

Don't go, Dad. Stay here with me. Oh, if only he would. I tried delaying tactics.

"Where is the market?"

"Not far from the corner, just down below. So hop to, Cinnamon, and let's get going."

"Yeah. You're slow as a slug," JoJo added.

I shoved JoJo ahead of me up the wide staircase.

"But I *am* dressed," he kept protesting.

"You have to put on your sandals."

"You could have brought them down."

"What am I? Your slave?" I *could* have brought them down, of course. But how could I go up there, past that rose room, alone? And wasn't that dumb! What a way to start off in a new house. "Hey, JoJo, close that door, will you?" I asked casually as we passed.

"What am I? Your slave?" JoJo wanted to know. But he pulled the door of the rose room shut and I let out my breath. Better. Definitely better. I could put a bolt on the outside of it. I'd tell Dad I was afraid of someone coming up through that empty space at night. And *that* was no lie. Glass *and* a bolt on the door. That would be better yet. But would glass and a bolt keep a ghost out? I didn't know about that, any more than I knew if there really was a ghost.

Dad was waiting for us as we came downstairs and we went out to the car.

I kept my head down, and I told myself that I wouldn't look along the curve of driveway. But I did. The oil stain from last night was still there, slick and shining, and behind it a few inches was a second one, wet and gleaming below the arch of the empty window. Two! Of course there would be two. He'd been back. I needed desperately to ask Dad and JoJo if they saw those two smears of oil, but I was afraid of what they'd say. And why was I so sure they'd say they saw nothing?

I made myself examine everything more carefully in the bright light of morning. The whole length of the driveway was pockmarked with old, dried stains. In places they'd blended together to make patches. The two fresh marks had started a second layer over the first. Had all the oil come from this same car? Had it sat there, night after night, waiting? If it did, it had stopped coming for a while and then started again when we came to stay. I shivered and craned my neck to look up at the empty window, at the sheer wall below it. There was a round flower bed directly beneath, a circle in the concrete filled with weeds.

JoJo tugged at my arm and pointed across the street. "That must be where Paul lives."

And Dad added, "Oh, yes, the boy who works in the pizza shop."

I was glad to look over at Paul's house. I was glad to think about Paul. Nice, normal, real Paul.

The house was big and wooden like ours, and set back behind a frazzled brown lawn. A swing hung from a thick branch of a tree and a small sting-ray bike lay by the steps that led to the overhang of the porch.

"Hey!" JoJo sat straight. "That's too *little* to be Paul's bike. He didn't say he had a brother. What age do you think he is, Cinnamon?"

"Maybe it's a kid sister," I said, and JoJo groaned.

"Not that! Not a dumb kid sister!"

Dad's eyes smiled at me in the rear-view mirror. His smile and the thought of Paul made the ghost image step back. I remembered Paul's dark hair, his broad shoulders. I remembered, too, the serious way he'd looked at me when he'd asked if there was anything wrong. Could I tell him? Oh, if only I could. I needed to talk to someone, someone who didn't know what had happened to me before. Somebody who wouldn't stare at me as if it were happening again. Hadn't Paul started to talk about the house too? It seemed to me he had, and then he'd stopped. Did he know something? I'd ask him.

"Look!" Dad slowed the car. "What a funny little place. I wonder who lives in it?"

We had just reached the bottom of the first dip, and there, snug at the foot of the Rookwood garden, was a wooden cottage. Its windows sparkled. The front door was painted a bright, sunny yellow. It had a small garden of its own, separated from the wilderness slope of the Rookwoods by a picket fence covered with honeysuckle. There were flowers everywhere. I saw tall hollyhocks, sweetpea and great clumps of white daisies.

"It's darling," I said. "Do you think someone really lives in it? It's so tiny."

"Somebody does," Dad said. "I never saw such a garden. There's everything in it. Marigolds, petunias . . ."

27

The word *roses* flashed into my mind. "I don't see any roses," I said.

"You're right. Seems to be everything but. Whoever lives here is definitely not big on roses."

"No." My heart was thumping. Every flower imaginable and not a single rose. Didn't most gardners like roses? And wouldn't they do well in the damp San Francisco weather? So? It meant nothing. Of course it meant nothing. I watched the little house through the car's back window till it disappeared from sight.

Now we could see the bay and across it the tall skyscrapers of San Francisco, shining in the pale sun.

"See the bridge, JoJo?" Dad asked. "And that's Alcatraz over there. Remember, we saw the light on it through the fog last night? They used to keep the worst criminals in the country there, but now the prison's empty and open for tours. We can go across some Saturday if you'd like."

I heard the change in Dad's voice as he began to speak again, and I knew that change. I call it his fake casual. The first couple of words in fake casual always make me stiffen.

"Oh, and by the way, Cinnamon . . ." *By the way* is usually how the fake casual starts. That phrase is a dead giveaway that something important is coming, something he doesn't want me to think is important. "By the way, they have a really first class ballet school in the city. It's run by a woman who was a prima ballerina with the Moscow ballet company. She's supposed to be excellent. Their quality is high. I thought you might be interested."

I stared out of the car window and heard the silence getting longer and longer. Little waves rippled against the promenade that ran the length of Sausalito's main street. A boy about JoJo's age was paddling, knee deep, pushing a toy sailboat into the water. "I'm not interested," I said.

"Well, if you change your mind . . ." Dad's fake casual trailed away.

I imagined him talking to Susan Shrink before we left. "If she could just get back into her ballet. I think it would really help her over this tough period."

And Susan Shrink saying, "Well, don't push it. Put the opportunity in front of her. But let the decision come from her."

I'd never change my mind. I'd never dance again. The desire had died in the plane crash along with Mom and Marissa. To give up dancing was my penance.

I'd been dumb enough to tell that to Susan Shrink once.

"You have nothing to do penance *for*. You made a reasonable choice. You didn't know what would happen."

Of course I hadn't known. But I knew now and I'd never dance again.

Dad swung into the parking lot of the Beach Market. It was early yet, and there were only two other cars in the marked stalls that faced the bay. Dad parked away from them, cut the engine and the three of us climbed out. It was so quiet that we could hear the water lapping on the shore.

I was slamming the car door when I heard someone pull into the space beside ours, and I moved quickly to get out of the way. Imagine, coming right next to us, I thought, when there's a whole empty parking lot.

I looked indignantly over my shoulder.

The motor was still running right next to me. But there was no car. As I stood, paralyzed, the motor cut to silence. Then I heard the first small plop of oil fall and I watched as it spread in a star-shaped stain, no bigger than a quarter in the middle of the marked rectangle, in the middle of the concrete emptiness.

Chapter 4

No," I said out loud. "What do you want? Leave me alone." I heard my voice rising, and at the same time, I heard a small gasp behind me. JoJo! I'd forgotten he was there.

Now he stood, staring at me, his eyes big, and scared in the littleness of his face.

"Cin . . . Cinnamon? What's the matter?"

"It's—" Couldn't he *see* that second small drop of oil that had just fallen from nothingness? He had to. I pointed. "Look at that!"

JoJo bent down and reached over. If there had been a real car there, he would have bumped metal. Now his head went through the ghost space. He picked up an old Snickers wrapper and held it out to me. "It's . . . only this, Cinnamon."

"Oh. For a minute I thought it was . . . You see, I thought I saw. . . ." I stopped. I was making it worse, babbling like a crazy person. It used to be, when I first got out of the hospital, that the kids at school never

ever said the word *crazy* in front of me. Maybe they'd been warned. Sometimes something would slip out, accidentally as in "That's crazy!" Or "Are you crazy?" Then there'd be a silence and somebody would nudge somebody else and nobody would look at me. *Oh, God! Was all that starting again?*

"What's keeping you two?" Dad called back over his shoulder.

JoJo dropped the wrapper, and I put my arm around his shoulder and hurried him forward, going wide around the car that I knew wasn't there. My mind scurried in all directions. The ghost was following me. It wasn't the house that was haunted then. I was the haunted one. Mom and Marissa? No, never. They'd never scare me like this.

JoJo squeezed my hand. "Cinnamon?" Little frightened voice. "Did you remember to put Fig Newtons on the list?"

I worked real hard on my smile. "I sure did, JoJo." I fished the list from my jeans pocket. "Look! Right on the top." Casual. As fake casual as Dad.

I walked up and down the market aisles with the others, pulling groceries from the shelves, tossing them into the metal cart. But my mind sputtered around. What I needed to do was make a list of what I had to find out. Susan Shrink says a list helps put your thoughts in order. Boy, did mine need some order. I'd get to it as soon as we got back. The very thought of going back to the house filled me with terror. The car would follow us, and I'd be alone except for JoJo. I wiped sweat from my forehead. No . . . I'd go across to Paul's, that's what I'd do. I'd see if he'd come over. But Paul would be working and . . .

"Hi, Cinnamon!" He was there, standing in the aisle in front of me as though I'd conjured him from my thoughts. Paul! I jumped and caught my breath.

"Geez! Did I scare you again? I seem to be always doing that."

"No. I was just thinking about you."

He raised his eyebrows and grinned. "Really?"

I felt my face flush. "I mean . . ."

"Hi, Paul," JoJo said. Dad smiled and said, "Not making pizzas this morning?"

"I don't start till two. Mom ran out of milk for breakfast, so I volunteered to come down for this."

For the first time I noticed the big plastic milk bottle he held. "It seemed only fair," he added, "since I polished off the last batch."

I realized I'd scarcely said a word. There were two cans of hot chili in the cart, and I picked one up in each hand and said, "Do you want to eat lunch with us? I mean, if you don't have anything better to do, and if you don't have to be at work till two. And if you like chili."

"Sure." Paul pointed. "I see you have crackers, too, so it's a deal."

"Have you got a little brother?" JoJo wanted to know.

"I have a big brother. He's in the Air Force so I don't see him too often. I have a little sister though."

"Bring her too." I was really looking at Paul for the first time. Last night didn't count. I'd been too frantic then to actually see him. He was maybe three inches taller than I, which isn't a bad height, since I'm five six. My height had always bugged me. That and being skinny. Then I'd started ballet, and what had been a pain turned out to be just right. I was pretty easy for the guys to lift for one thing. Of course, being right for ballet didn't matter anymore. Paul was thin, too, as I could plainly see since he was wearing only raggedy cutoff jeans and beach walkers. Thin and very brown. Last night, under the lamplight, I'd thought his hair was black. But I'd been fooled by the shadows. It was brown, too, just a shade darker than his skin, and his eyes had a golden look to them. Lion eyes. I wondered if he was strong. You could be thin and strong at the same time, like a dancer. It would be nice to have someone strong around in case the ghost came.

I shook my head.

"No?" Paul asked.

"No, what?"

"You shook your head about something."

I managed a smile. "Not really."

"Well, I'd better get going," Paul said. "Everything has come to a sudden halt at home, waiting for the milk delivery."

"We'll be through in a minute if you want a ride back," Dad offered.

"Thanks. But I have my mom's car." Paul shifted the milk from one hand to another, tossing it like a ball. "See you later then."

"Come early," I said. "Come as early as you can. Right after breakfast would be okay." Gag! Did I sound eager! What on earth would he think? But I didn't care. "Will you come right away?"

Paul's smile faded. "Sure," he said slowly, "whenever you like."

I tried for a normal voice. Don't scare him off,

Cinnamon. If he thinks you're weird he'll disappear on you. People do. I knew that.

"See you," I said.

We were almost finished with the marketing ourselves.

While the checker rang up the huge grocery order from the two carts, I moved a little so I could see out of the plate glass window to the parking lot. Was the ghost car still there? I couldn't tell, of course. If it was, I was looking right through it at the ocean behind, where a flock of gulls wheeled and somersaulted against the wash of sky. Please be gone, I begged it. Don't do this to me anymore.

But it was there. The oil stains were larger where it had waited, crouched in the empty stall. Where it had waited for me.

As we left I rolled down my window and heard the ghost motor start behind us. I heard it follow us up the hill, past the little flower house, up the last dip in the roller coaster road to the Rookwood driveway. It parked right behind us, and its motor shut off a few seconds after ours.

I opened the door of our car and rushed up the steps to the front porch without even waiting for a single bag of groceries. My hand shook so much that I could hardly get the key in the lock.

"Hey! Cinnamon!" JoJo called. "That's no fair. Come back and carry something, you lazy pig."

"It's okay," Dad said. "We'll tote it in and she'll unpack it. How's that? You can eat Fig Newtons and watch her work."

"Yeah!" JoJo said.

I waited for them in the kitchen, feeling safer somehow than outside. I didn't want to examine that thought, for fear it made no sense. What did ghosts know of doors or walls?

I made coffee for Dad before he took off for work. It's amazing how a person can function even when her mind is somewhere else. In my head I made lists. If I could get started doing something to make sense of all this I might feel better.

I pretended to be too busy unpacking food to see Dad off, and I warned JoJo twice about making sure he locked the front door when he came back inside. I had to hold on to my faith in locked doors. There wasn't anything else.

JoJo was watching TV, and I'd started on my lists when the doorbell rang. JoJo charged past me to open it.

I grabbed his arm and swung him to a stop.

"Careful, JoJo. See who it is before you open it."

JoJo gave me a look of contempt. "Faddle, Cinnamon! Do you think I'm going to let Jack the Ripper in? Or Dracula?" He shook away my hand.

I jumped up. "No. Wait. I'll go." Scared or not, I couldn't let JoJo be the one to open that door with the ghost waiting outside.

It was Paul. Paul! I was so glad to see him I could have thrown my arms around him.

"Hi!"

"Hi." I closed and locked the door again.

"Is ten thirty too early for chili?" he asked.

"Maybe," I said. "But it's not too early for a cold drink. Where's your little sister?"

"Little sister!" JoJo repeated disgustedly.

"She wouldn't come. She says, 'Who needs boys?' She says she'd have come if JoJo were a girl. She says that boys stink. She says she wouldn't be caught dead going over to a boy's house. She says, anyway, she'd rather stay home and play Pac Man. She says . . ." He stopped and grinned. "Get the drift?"

"She's got Pac Man? The real one that you play on the TV?" JoJo didn't seem to have heard anything else. "Gee! Could I go over there?"

"Sure," Paul said. "Her name's Donna. My mom calls her Madonna because she thinks she's an angel. The rest of us call her Belladonna."

JoJo wrinkled his nose. "What's that?"

"It's a poison. So better watch out."

"Pac Man! Gee!" was all JoJo said, and rushed back to the front door.

"Wait!" I had a sudden vision of him passing that car and a ghostly hand coming out to drag him inside where he'd be gone forever. "Wait, JoJo." My heart was hammering. "Look, that's a busy street. I'll just walk you across."

JoJo rolled his eyes. "Oh, faddle twaddle! There's not even a *car* on that street. What do you think I am, a *baby?*" And he was gone, the door slamming behind him.

I watched from the window till he was safely across. I watched him through the transparency of the ghost car that I knew was still there.

"He's right, you know," Paul said behind me. "There's really not much traffic up here at all. I don't think you have to worry about him."

Oh, no? I thought. But I said nothing. I was suddenly so cold that I hugged my arms around myself as we walked back to the kitchen.

Paul stood by the table. "Are you writing letters already?"

"Uh-uh." I turned the top list face down. "I've been making a note of things I want to ask you, in case I'd forget any of them. I hope you don't mind. I *like* to make lists," I added lamely.

"Boy, what organization! You mean, like who has the best ice cream in town and where do the kids hang out . . . stuff like that?"

"Kind of." I fished out the list I'd made for him and said, "Here!"

While he read I went to the refrigerator and got the apple juice. I poured two glasses and watched him secretly. This list was going to throw him. I wasn't exactly asking about ice cream. What *would* he think? He'd put on a wrinkled blue T-shirt with his cutoffs, which was probably his idea of dressing for lunch. Definitely strong, I decided. Those were muscles all right at the top of his arms moving under the tight cotton T-shirt.

"Gee!" he muttered at last and looked up. "You certainly want to get to know about a place fast." He slid the paper across the table. "You have to admit, some of these questions are pretty strange."

"I know. I'll try to explain later." I took a sip of my juice and had trouble swallowing it. How much should I try explaining? And if he thought the questions were weird, what would he think about the explanation? "Can you . . . answer them? Do you mind? Please, Paul."

"I'll do my best." He pulled the sheet of paper toward him again. "How long have we lived here? Let me see, three years. Belladonna was three, and I was just starting high school. There's quite a gap between the kids in my family. In yours, too, I guess."

"I had a sister between me and JoJo," I said. "She was killed last year."

"Geez!" Paul's hand touched mine briefly. "That's tough. I'm sorry."

"My mom too," I said stiffly. "Plane accident."

Paul pushed his chair so it swayed on its back legs. His voice was soft. "That's terrible. I wondered about your mom. I thought maybe your parents were divorced."

"No." I took another sip of juice. "So you've lived here three years. Do you know the Rookwoods well?"

"Uh-uh. They're artists. They're a bit, well, arty, I guess. And they keep to themselves. They're in their fifties. No kids. She's Georgette and he's Robert."

Paul looked down at the list and smiled. "Who lives in the little house below? Mrs. Nellie Cram. Now *she's* been here for ever and ever. She came to Sausalito as a bride. Her husband was a seafaring man, very handsome, as she's certain to tell you. She's been a widow for about thirty years, but she still raves about what a fine physique he had. How gallant he was. Her words, not mine. It's kind of nice."

"Is she okay? I mean, do you get along with her?"

"She's super. And she makes the best blueberry muffins ever. I'll take you down to meet her."

"She doesn't have any roses in her garden," I said.

"Roses?" Paul looked baffled. "She has to have. She has *everything* in that garden."

"No roses."

"Huh! Well, I never noticed."

"What about the girl who lived here last summer? You said there was one. Alison, was it?" I leaned forward and pointed to question three.

"There were two girls, actually. Alison came after Lisa. Lisa Berringer. She was only here for about a week."

"Oh?" I sat forward. My heart was doing strange things, wheeling inside me the way the gulls had wheeled this morning against the sky. "That seems strange. Nobody moves into a house like this for a week, surely?"

"No. Her father took the place for three months the way all the Rookwood summer renters do. They'd paid and everything. That's what Georgette Rookwood told my mom when she and Robert got back from Europe. They were mad at first, because they didn't want the house lying empty. But the real estate people who handle the place for them rented it to another family, so the Rookwoods made out good in the end. Six months' rent for three months' wear and tear."

"But do you know *why* they left? The first people?"

"I've no idea. I know Lisa didn't like the house from the start. But that doesn't seem much of a reason to abandon it."

"Did she tell you why she didn't like it?"

Paul shook his head. "She was a real strange girl. Donna called her 'Loony Lisa.' I'd guess she was into drugs and a bunch of other stuff. Maybe it was just too square for her around here."

"Where did they go?"

40

"Back to Ohio, I guess. Her dad was some sort of professor at Ohio State."

"You didn't write to her or ask or anything?"

Paul shook his head. "I hardly knew her. I think I only talked to her twice. Once she said, 'This is a far-out house, man, and I mean far out!' She looked even wackier than usual that day. But with someone like that, who knows?"

Someone like that, I thought. *Someone strange. Someone wacky. Me and Loony Lisa. And if I told you there was something wrong with this house would you think I was weird too? I just bet you would.*

"What about the other girl? Alison? You said she came after Lisa left. Did she say anything about the house?"

"Nothing, really. Except that she hated the hill. Alison was into jogging, and that hill is the pits. Alison Burch is her name."

"Do you know where she lives?"

"Sure. 3649 Fourth Street, Milwaukee, Wisconsin."

"I gather she wasn't wacky or any of those things," I said and Paul grinned. "Super normal."

I bet she was good-looking, I thought. But I didn't ask. "Do you have her phone number, too, by any chance?"

"Naturally."

"Naturally," I repeated. Alison had definitely been a fox.

I turned over my list and wrote her address and the phone number Paul knew by heart on the back. Then I wrote Lisa's name and the words *Ohio State*. She shouldn't be that hard to track.

Paul was watching me over the rim of his juice glass.

"Have I answered everything?" He bent over the list. "No, Cinnamon, I never heard a car turn in the driveway and just sit." His head lifted. "And don't you mean have I ever *seen* a car? You have a strange way of putting that. Anyway, I haven't." He pushed the list away. "Last question. Have *I* ever heard anything strange about the house?" He stopped and poured more juice. I sensed his hesitation.

"Well?" My heart was doing all those weird things again.

"Not really. Not *strange* as in creepy. But yes, there is one little thing. It's nothing . . . I almost told you last night."

"Hurry up! What?" I hadn't meant to sound so sharp.

"You want me to show you?"

"Show me? Where is it?"

Paul stood. "Is it okay if I go upstairs?"

I nodded and stood too. It was something upstairs. I knew where.

I followed Paul through the kitchen and hallway and up the wide quiet staircase. Sunlight lay in cheerful splotches on the golden wood. The Rookwood paintings were bright, jungle colors against the white walls.

Paul stopped at the top of the stairs.

"Wait a sec. Which is the room with the arched window?" His hand lifted. "This one. Right?"

"Yes." The word got caught somewhere in my throat.

He opened the door.

From behind him I could see the pink emptiness of the room. The books were piled on the floor as I had left them. I saw the valentine card on top of the torn picture. The empty arch of window framed the trees across the street.

Paul walked across the room.

"Do you know why there's no glass in this window?"

"No." I hovered by the door.

"Because glass won't stay in it, that's why. It has something to do with the arch not being symmetrical and the contraction of the wooden frame. Robert Rookwood told my dad. They had a glass company come out two or three times, and each time the window shattered in about a million pieces as soon as it was in. Weird, huh?" He turned to face me. Sunlight made a halo around him. "Once I was in our back yard, and I heard this thing smash. Geez! Talk about an explosion!"

I stood, frozen. It had nothing to do with the arch not being symmetrical. I knew that. *He* didn't want glass in that window. He wouldn't have it.

"The Rookwoods decided it was too dangerous, so they never tried again," Paul said. He was leaning through the open arch, running his hands around the window frame. "Here's something strange! I wonder when this was done?"

"What?" I'd taken a step back into the safety of the hallway.

"Come and look," Paul said glancing over his shoulder.

What else? What now? Slowly I moved through the doorway and into the rose room.

Chapter 5

"Look!" Paul said. "You can see that the window was once barred. There's a hole here at the top and a matching one below." He counted places where four bars had been, two long ones in the middle, two shorter on either side. "They were thick sons of guns too," Paul said. "Somebody must have had something valuable in here once upon a time."

"Yes." I touched one of the empty holes with my fingertips. Bars to keep someone in. Or someone out.

I leaned forward a little and looked down into the sunlit driveway. Was the ghost there, sitting patiently in the ghost car, waiting? Ghosts had all the time in the world to wait. All the time through eternity. I shivered and pulled back.

"Cold?" Paul asked.

"No. Someone walking on my grave."

Paul stared around. "Are you going to take this room? It looks as if you've started clearing stuff out. You could fix it up really nice."

"No," I said. "I don't like that window. Mosquito bites aren't my favorite things."

"Yeah." Paul wasn't really listening and I saw that he was looking at the valentine card that I'd left face down on top of the picture. He walked across and picked it up. "Is this yours?"

"No. I found it in the back of that print." I felt myself cringe as Paul turned the card over, looking at the drawing of the half-opened rose. I waited for the sick sweetness of the perfume to fill the room again, for the floating dizziness to come. But nothing happened, and I let out my breath.

"My dark and lovely valentine," Paul read. "It *could* have been yours. You fit the description."

"It's not mine."

Paul smiled and picked up the companion picture I'd taken from the wall. "Do you think there's something in the back of this one, too?" He flipped a hand toward the others, still hanging. "There could be something in all of them. People did that. They used to hide gold certificates and all kinds of things. Treasure. Should we look?"

"Well . . ."

"How about this one, then?" The serious kid in his father's boots disappeared as Paul turned the picture face down. "The backing's almost off anyway."

"Go ahead." How cool I was! No one would have guessed how hard a time I was having just breathing. There *would* be something behind this one. I knew it. I glanced over my shoulder at the empty window and moved out of its range.

Paul's fingers slipped under the tape and stripped it away. The paper came off in two crumbling pieces.

45

"Aha!" Paul darted a conspiratorial look in my direction. Below I saw a yellowed card with writing on it.

Paul lifted it out, bent down to set the second backless picture on top of the other one, and straightened up.

Another card, I thought and tensed. But it wasn't a card. Paul turned it over and I saw a photograph. He held it so I could see it better. A boy and girl walked along a wide sidewalk that edged an ocean. The girl licked at an ice cream cone. Behind them, in the water, swimmers splashed and a man stood upright in a rowboat.

I moved a step closer. The girl had long, curling black hair that hung below her shoulders. She wore a dark cotton peasant skirt with three tiers, and a light blouse that had an eyelet frill at the neck. Her shoes were white and laced—saddle shoes, I guess, and she wore anklets.

He was even darker than she was, dark of hair, dark of skin. Spanish maybe or Italian. His dress pants had pleats in the front and his shirt looked like silk. His feet were cut out of the picture. A sailor's cap with a peak was perched at a rakish angle on his head. He smiled at the photographer, and the girl's eyes sparkled and danced above the ice cream cone.

"Some fancy threads he's wearing," Paul said. "The guy was a flash dresser whoever he was."

It was a wonderful picture. I'd never ever seen such joy. You wanted to reach out and touch it, and be part of it.

"Probably one of those street photographers," Paul

went on. "You know, you pay a dollar and pick it up later? I'd say there were no Polaroids then. How long ago do you think this was? Maybe forty years?"

He turned the picture over and said, "Here it is. FELIX AND I, JUNE 1937."

"Felix!" I said.

"Here!" Paul held it out. "I think it was taken in Sausalito. See! That looks just like the edge of Alcatraz in the right-hand corner and . . ." He stopped. "What's the matter? Cinnamon? Are you all right?"

The photograph in my hand was growing larger and larger, rising to float in front of me. I saw the two faces bigger than life-size. The waffle design on the cone was as big as the squares on a checker board. I saw every minute freckle on the girl's face, the little dancing flecks in her dark eyes. I saw a mole, small and golden, in the hollow of Felix's throat, and all around me was the rose smell, suffocating me, drowning me. I felt myself swaying, and then Paul's arms were around me, holding me tight. My fingers loosened their grip on the photograph that was too heavy to hold, and it dropped to the floor.

"Cinnamon? Cinnamon? What's the matter?"

I had my eyes tightly closed, my face pressed against his T-shirt.

"It's . . . it's . . ." *Oh, no! Don't let me cry! If I cry . . .*

But I was crying, big muffled, gulpy sobs.

Paul patted my shoulder. I could feel him standing there, stiff and awkward, probably wishing he'd never heard of me. Probably wondering how he'd gotten into this and how he could get out.

I pulled back. "I'm sorry. The picture . . . it . . ."

"Did the girl . . . remind you of your sister, or something?"

I shook my head. It would be so easy to say yes. People forgave you for freaking out over someone dying. Freaking out was even expected. For a while. But I couldn't bring myself to use Marissa this way. "No. It's just that I still . . . cry easily over things." I tried to smile.

"Well, you sure scared me. You looked as if you'd seen a ghost." He bent down and picked up the photograph. It was regular size for me now too, and the rose smell had vanished.

I watched as Paul put it on top of the picture on the floor and then I watched as his mind reached for something better and I saw him slip it underneath, out of my sight. Nice Paul!

I touched his arm. "I'm sorry about that."

"Hey! It was nothing. Crying's healthy." His face was serious. "I keep reading that. It's better than bottling things up."

"I know." Boy, did I know! Bottling it up had been my trouble, right from the start. It was Dad who told me Mom and Marissa had been killed. He told JoJo and me separately. I don't know how he handled it with JoJo, but with me he hugged me and said, "Cinnamon? Cinnamon, love? Mom and Marissa are gone."

"Gone? I know they're gone." I'd laughed. "What are you talking about? Have you forgotten I went to the airport with you?"

"That's not what I mean. Oh, Cinnamon! Their

plane crashed on landing. There were no survivors."

"Gone!" I said. "Gone?" I kept saying it and saying it. Dad's face. It had shrunk to half its size. Tears dripped down his cheeks and plopped onto the front of his shirt. His black tie had wet marks on it.

"Gone?" I said.

I should have known something drastic had happened. But I hadn't. I'd been in rehearsal when Colette had sent for me. When I got to her office she said, "You must go home right away, *ma chérie*. Your father says you should take a taxi, and that I should ascertain if you have sufficient money." Colette, who after all this time still sounded like a Frenchwoman whose English was too correct.

"I have money. But why does he want me home now? And why shouldn't I go on the bus, the way I always do?"

"It would be best, perhaps, just to do as he requests. Doubtless your father has a convincing reason."

I should have known something drastic had happened. But I didn't. They're going to call as soon as they arrive at Aunt Clara's, I thought. Dad forgot to tell me. He wants me there.

"Gone," I'd whispered.

"We have to help each other, Cinnamon," Dad said. "We have to be strong together."

But Marissa shouldn't even have been there. She went instead of me. And Mom. I'd talked her into the whole thing.

Dad was reading my mind. "Cinnamon. Lovey. You

49

didn't know. Nobody blames you. *They* wouldn't. Cinnamon . . .''

I had been strong. Hadn't I done enough? Mom and Marissa were dead because of me. Dad was like this because of me. The least I could do was be strong. I didn't cry. I didn't cry at the memorial service when Mom's friends stood and said wonderful things about her, and when Marissa's fifth grade class sang "You Light Up My Life," her all-time favorite.

Five weeks later, when school started again after summer, I'd heard Debbie Valdez say to Jenny: "Cinnamon Cameron's weird. If my mom and sister were killed, I'd have cried buckets. Wouldn't you, Jen? She never cried at all. Jim Gallagher said he even heard her laugh once. That was days later, of course, but still. Can you imagine? She acts as if she doesn't care." They were in the bathroom, fixing their hair, and they didn't know I was behind one of the closed doors.

"She has to be weird," Jenny said. "Even I cried and she wasn't *my* mother." Jenny said that. Jenny, my best friend.

I stayed behind that door all through fifth period.

They probably thought I was weirder the day in English class when everything broke inside me, and I began screaming and punching at Mr. Penrose when he came to comfort me. They *knew* I was weird then, all right.

Susan Shrink said I shouldn't have tried to be brave. Not crying was definitely part of my problem.

I didn't know how long I'd been standing there with my hand on Paul's arm, going over it and over it again in my head. Too long.

50

I stepped back and wiped my eyes with my hand. "Yeah. Crying must be healthy. I feel better, anyway."

"You know what I think?" Paul said. "I think it's chili time."

I nodded. "Definitely."

"You're going to have to learn California-speak if you plan on living here," Paul said. "Around these parts we say *for sure.*"

"Okay. For sure, then." I knew he was trying to cheer me up, and I recognized fake casual in his voice and in the way he closed the door of the rose room behind us. One thing I was very good at was recognizing fake casual.

We went down the stairs side by side.

I told myself I wouldn't think about the photograph and Felix and the girl. But my mind kept switching to them and my body kept reacting with little shakes and shivers.

Paul opened the chili and put it on to heat while I set out bowls and napkins. Chili! The very thought of it made me ill. "Smells good," I said. I was getting to be a fine liar too. I struggled for ordinary talk. "Should I call your mom and have her send JoJo home for lunch? I don't want him to be a pest on his first day."

"If he likes peanut butter, banana and marshmallow sandwiches on whole wheat, leave him alone. That's what he'll have over there. That's what Belladonna has every day of her little life."

"He'll be in heaven," I said.

Paul ate and I tried to look as if I were eating, which isn't easy. Paul talked.

He told me that his dad was a hospital administrator

51

in the big Kaiser Hospital in San Francisco. His mom taught second grade in Sausalito.

"Just her luck, she'll be having Belladonna in her class next year. Can you imagine, being the teacher and having to confess that that little monster is *yours*?"

He told me he would be starting San Francisco State University in September. Maybe he wanted to be an architect. He didn't know for sure.

I was terribly aware of the wall clock behind him, the hands getting closer and closer to the time when he'd have to go. And when he went I'd be alone again. I couldn't be. I'd go out, somewhere, anywhere. But then, I'd have to pass the car . . .

"Are you okay, Cinnamon?"

"I'm fine." *Don't let him see. Don't start off here being weird, too.*

Paul leaned across the table and his hand covered mine. Freaked out as I was, I still liked how it felt, warm and strong. I looked down and saw the little pale hairs that ran up from his wrist to the smoothness of his arm. My heart began to race, but this time it was for a nice, normal reason. Did he like me, just a bit? Even if I did seem spacey and strange?

"Look, Cinnamon," he said softly. "I'd have to be dumb not to know something is really bugging you. It has to do with this house, hasn't it? I know you're still upset over your mom and sister. How could you not be? But there's something else too. All those questions! Why don't you tell me? I'm good with secrets, honest!"

If only I could. I looked up into those golden eyes,

and my heart quickened even more. His eyebrows were thick and a bit ruffled. If he were a girl he'd probably have arched them or something and that would have been a shame. I wanted to smooth them with a fingertip, to touch his face.

"Don't you want to tell me?" he asked. "Telling's healthy too."

I smiled. "For sure." But I couldn't tell him. Loony Lisa and Crazy Cinnamon. "She's off her hinges," I'd heard one of the kids at school say as I passed.

"Ssh! It's because her mom and sister were killed. She's entitled to be off her hinges, you nut."

"Yeah. But that was more than a year ago now. Come on!"

I slid my hand out from under Paul's. "It's really nothing. Just a few things I need to work out for myself."

Paul shrugged. "Well, I'll be around. Right now I've got to split. But you know what? Tomorrow's my day off. If I can pry Mom's car away from her . . ." He stopped and grinned. "And I usually can if I've got a real important reason."

Like a girl, I thought. I wonder if she lent you her car for Alison? But I wasn't crazy enough to mess things up by saying something like that. Craziness only goes so far.

"Anyway, if she'll give it to me, would you like to go sightseeing? There are lots of nice places around here. We could go to Bolinas, to the beach and—"

"I'd love to." Gag! I should have at least let him finish. But a whole day away from this house, away from the ghost room and the ghost car. Wouldn't *it* follow us, though? I wouldn't think about that. I'd think about one thing at a time.

"Great," he said. "I'm glad you'd love to."

"What about JoJo?"

"JoJo, too, of course. Unless we can pursuade him to stay with Belladonna. If he survived her today maybe he could take another session."

Paul was standing. The clock on the wall said one twenty. I knew he had to go.

"I'll fix a picnic for tomorrow," I said. "What kind of sandwiches? Not marshmallow and peanut butter, I hope."

"Anything else! I'll call you when I get home from work tonight, just to be certain I can have the car."

"Can we do something else if you don't? Walk somewhere? Take a bus?" The words jumped out of my desperation. I didn't think I could stand it if I had to be here tomorrow. But I couldn't go every day. I had to get to the bottom of this thing, find out if it were real. . .

"For sure. Or *fur shur,* as you say if you're *truly* a native." We were standing now by the closed and locked front door.

"Cinnamon?" Paul ran his hand through the thickness of his hair. "I'm glad you want to go tomorrow. But why am I still getting these uneasy vibes? You want to go because . . . well, maybe you'll tell me tomorrow."

"Maybe." But I knew I wouldn't. I opened the door cautiously. There was nothing in the driveway.

"Oh," I said. "You'd better send JoJo home. And Donna, too, if she wants to come for a while." Send everybody, I thought.

"You want to borrow my dog?" How *could* this guy be reading my thoughts.

"You have a dog?" What a wonderful thought. Maybe Dad would let *us* get a dog. . . I clasped my hands together. "Oh, I'd love him. For company, you know. Just till we get settled. But would he stay?"

"Jasper will stay with anyone. He's kind of fat and useless. But adorable. He'll think he's on vacation. He's pretty dumb, actually."

"Oh, Paul. That would be so wonderful."

"I'll bring him with us tomorrow. You can get acquainted. Then you can take him for as long as you want."

Nice Paul. Oh, nice, nice Paul.

"I'll talk to you later," he said. "Okay?"

"Okay."

I watched him go down the steps in two jumps, stride to the wall and vault across. Then I stood for a few seconds in the safety of the doorway and scanned the drive. Nothing. Three oil splotches, that was all. No new drops falling. No motor noise. Nothing.

My hand tightened on the doorknob. Could he have given up? Could he have decided I didn't have whatever it was he wanted? Had he gone away? Oh, pray he had. Please! I took a hesitant step onto the porch and heard the engine start with a roar. Vroom! Vroom!

I jerked my head around and saw it. Saw it! My hands jammed against my mouth. The motor stopped as suddenly as it had begun, and I realized it had started only to get my attention.

There it sat, outlined the way a child would trace around a picture with a thick, black pencil. I saw the car's long angled shape. Transparent though. Empty in the middle. And I backed up. The edge of the open front door jarred between my shoulders sending its warning shock all the way down my back.

It was still there then. Still waiting.

Chapter 6

 I huddled at the kitchen table. Oh, if only Mom were here! And Marissa! Marissa would have believed me even if she couldn't see the things I saw and couldn't hear the things I heard. I had never felt so alone.

The refrigerator hummed as the thermostat came on. The big hand of the clock reached the half hour and clicked.

I needed to go to the bathroom. But the only bathroom was upstairs, and I wasn't going back upstairs.

The empty chili bowls still sat on the table. So did the lists and my pad of paper. I pushed the dishes aside and tore off another sheet from the pad. Susan Shrink was right. It did help to put things down. I made a heading, "PEOPLE I COULD TALK TO ABOUT THIS." Then I wrote "Dad," and beside that, "No. Worry him to death. He'll think I've gone off the deep end again. He'll call Susan Shrink for advice or fake casual me into going to somebody just like her."

Anyway, poor, sad Dad has enough to worry about. "Susan Shrink? No. She might call Dad. See above."

Paul? I sat chewing on the top of my pencil, my mind on what I was doing, but every sense alert for a noise or movement inside or outside the house. There was none.

Paul was nice. But would he believe me? If *I* wasn't sure of the reality, how could he be sure? It could be like pointing to myself and saying, "See me? Maybe I'm still flipped out."

I put the pencil down, then picked it up again.

"Paul's mother? Or Mrs. Cram?" First I'd need to meet them and check them out.

"Lisa Berringer? Alison?" If I were real careful, super careful, I could call them both and question them about the house without their getting suspicious. And I could do it right away.

The Rookwood phone was red and hung on the wall by the kitchen table. I direct-dialed the long distance number Paul had given me for Alison.

I guess it was her brother who answered and who shouted her name in that nasty way brothers always do. "Alison! Phone! Yes, it's for you. If it was for me, would I be yelling for you to come?"

The receiver dropped on a table or something with a clang that almost took my ear off, and I heard Alison's faint voice call, "Who is it, Duff?"

"It's not a boy, if that's what you mean."

I imagined her running through some anonymous house in her jogging suit, all pink and healthy and windblown.

"Hi!" Breathless voice.

"Hi! My name is Cinnamon Cameron. I'm living in

58

the house in Sausalito where you stayed last summer?"

"Oh, yeah?" I could sense her wondering *what is this?* "So. . . how's the house?" she asked.

"It's okay, I guess. I wondered, when you stayed here, what did you think of it?" Gag! I should have taken more time and practiced this. She'd think I was *crazy.* And there was that awful word again.

"It was all right." Pause. "I like to run and the hills were a pain."

"I know. Paul told me."

More pause. "How is Paul?"

"He's fine." Something was humming between us.

"Funny, I talked to him a couple of days ago. He didn't say anything about new people in the Rookwood house."

"We just got here." So she'd talked to him a couple of days ago? I wondered what she looked like. Was she blond? Tall? Probably a super figure with all that running. Well, dancers had okay figures too. Not that I was a dancer any more. Funny to think she might be wondering what *I* looked like. The unknown competition. But that was ridiculous. We weren't in competition. I hardly knew Paul.

"You know the room with the arched window?" I asked. "You didn't sleep in there, did you?"

Normal laugh. Nothing hidden, nothing secretive, nothing frightened. "Are you kidding? You mean in Emily's room? I wouldn't sleep in there if you paid me! Too many spiders and prehistoric dust. Probably mice, too, with that crazy open window. None of us used it."

I tried to keep my voice cool. "Who's Emily?"

"Oh, I guess you haven't been there long enough to start poking around. Those boxes and trunks and things are full of her stuff."

I saw my knuckles, white against the red lacquer of the phone. "No. I haven't seen anything. But do you know who she is?"

"I'd say she's in the past tense. She lived in the house, I guess, a long time ago. In fact, there's an old yearbook of hers in one of the trunks. I forget the date."

I leaned my head against the cool, white wall. There was a small, hairline crack in the paint, and I traced it with my finger.

"What happened to her? Do you know?"

I could almost hear the shrug in Alison's voice. "Who knows? Whatever happened, she left pretty fast. Everything's in those trunks, even her underwear. It's as if she packed for a trip and never went. My brother says she probably fell out of that stupid window, splat, onto the driveway." She giggled. "Duff has a morbid imagination."

Maybe she sensed my shock. Her voice changed. "Say. I'm just remembering. You know the worst thing about that house? That one bathroom! I mean, who ever heard of one bathroom with five bedrooms? We had fights over that place everyday."

I turned around and leaned against the wall. She didn't know anything more. I needed to get this over with now, graciously. "It was nice talking to you, Alison."

"You know about the other girl, don't you?"

"Lisa?"

"That's the one. I thought I should just mention her."

"Yes. Well, thanks a lot."

"For what? Are you doing a summer project on the house or something like that."

"Yes. Something like that."

"Tell Paul I said hello. And tell him I'll see him real soon."

"Oh? Is he. . .going to visit you over the summer?"

"Uh-uh. I'm coming there. In the fall. I'll be at Berkeley. Tell him to be good till I get there."

"I'll tell him," I said. "Bye, Alison."

"Bye . . . uh . . . uh. . . Nice talking to you." I could tell she'd forgotten my name.

I hung the phone back on its silvery hook. She'd be here. So what? With any luck, I wouldn't. I sat at the table where Paul had sat.

Upstairs, in those trunks and boxes, were things that had belonged to Emily. Was Emily the girl in the picture? The dark and lovely valentine? What had happened to her? Could *she* be the driver of the ghost car? I'd always thought of a *he*. I needed to go up there now and search for something that would help me understand.

I poured the last of the apple juice into my used glass and saw my hand shake as I lifted it to drink. Up there! Up and into the rose room. But. . .I remembered, the trunks weren't in there. JoJo and I had moved all of them. They sat on the floor of Marissa's room. It would be safe in there, wouldn't it? I'd noticed a nice little bolt on the door. I could slide it across and nothing could get at me.

First I would try to find Lisa.

Information gave me the number for Ohio State University, and I dialed the operator and asked for a person-to-person call with Professor Berringer.

It took forever, shifting from department to department. Once we got disconnected and the exasperated operator muttered at me that wouldn't you know it, and to hold on, she'd try again. At last a man said this was Professor Berringer's office, but the professor wasn't in at the moment. Did I want him to return my call? The operator left the number. The professor would probably have a fit when he discovered it was a California number.

"Tell him to call collect," I said. And Dad would have a fit when he saw these weird phone bills. I'd have trouble explaining.

But now I'd done what I had to do, and there was no excuse left not to face what lay upstairs.

I went quickly, so I wouldn't have time to think. My feet clattered and echoed on the wooden stairs and my blood pounded and echoed somewhere, too, somewhere inside the hollowness of my chest. Fast into the bathroom, because I couldn't wait any longer, fast into Marissa's bedroom, trembling fingers shooting across the little bolt, turning to see the two big trunks with their rusted metal bands waiting on the wooden floor. I stood to let my breath slow. There was nothing frightening in here. Birds chirped outside the windows. An airplane droned high overhead. Nice woodsy chest and dresser. Nice little bed under the slope of the ceiling. Everything cluttered now with the extra stuff. The trunks. Old-fashioned. Harmless.

I knelt beside the largest one. Its top was a rounded

hump, and when I undid the hasps and opened it, I saw that there were two levels of storage. On the top was a full-sized lid, about four inches deep. Underneath it would be the depth of the trunk. There was a lingering smell of mothballs.

Along the lid was spread a dress that had once been white. Now it was yellowed and fragile-looking. I guessed that if Alison had disturbed this, she had put it back exactly as she'd found it. It looked like a wedding dress, but something told me it wasn't. There was a young, party-going feel to it. A prom dress maybe? Graduation? I lifted up the drift of skirt and saw white satin pumps underneath and a small beaded purse. Carefully I removed the entire tray and set it on the bed.

Underneath were folded sweaters and skirts. When I eased them up, I saw other clothes below. Underwear, as Alison had said. A robe. Shoes. White saddle shoes. I ruffled through the things above, knowing what I would find before I found it. The tiered peasant skirt! It was brown, and the blouse that she'd worn with it was cream, not white, as I'd thought it was in the picture. I sat back on my heels. Where was the yearbook? Not in here. I put the long tray back and closed the lid.

The smaller trunk had a flat top. The yearbook was the first thing I saw when I opened it. It was lying next to a pink satin case with *Pyjamas* embroidered on the front. There was a music box, still wound up enough after all this time to play a few bars of a Viennese waltz when I lifted its lid. The tinkling sound spooked me. Someone's fingers had wound this once. Someone had hummed to the melody, way, way before I was born.

I picked up the book. It was green leather and had a round, embossed seal on the front. Underneath, in gold letters, it said MARIN COUNTY HIGH SCHOOL, 1937. In smaller gold print it said EMILY McWHIRTER.

I sat on the edge of the bed with the book on my knees. As soon as I looked in here, there would be more of that floating awfulness. But there was no other way. I felt as I'd felt once, standing at the top of a high diving board looking into the water below. Kids crowded behind me and there was no way down except to jump. I jumped then. I jumped now.

The yearbook opened where books usually open, at the most looked at place. I knew what I would see, and I saw it. There were four rectangles on each facing page. Boys on the right, girls on the left. Eight faces smiled up at me. Above, in large print it said AND CONGRATULATIONS TO THESE MEMBERS OF THE GRADUATING CLASS OF '37. I saw Emily instantly and I saw Felix. They were placed directly opposite one another, and I had the immediate thought that when the book was closed, those two faces had been pressed together for all those years.

She wore a blouse with a little round collar, and there was a broad band of ribbon holding back her hair. His shirt was short-sleeved and checked. He leaned forward eagerly into the camera. The same sailor's cap was tilted at the same impossible angle on his dark hair. Someone had penciled inside a small heart in the whiteness of the square next to him the words *Felix Ferrero and Emily McWhirter*.

Under her name it said: "Emily the librarian? Here is one gal who likes books more than boys. Uh, well, anyway, she *does* like books." Under his: "Felix tells us he wouldn't be caught dead without his yachting cap. Anyone for sailing?"

At first I thought it was my hands that were trembling. Then I realized it was the book. Great shivers, like electric shocks, ran through it. I dropped it on the bed and jumped up. I should run, hide, get away from here. But I couldn't move. The book shuddered and spasmed. The air from its fluttering pages fanned up and around me. There was the faint, faraway drift of roses. I pressed my hands against my face. Stop! Stop. It was stopping, the pages flapping like a dying bird. Now it lay, still and lifeless on the bed.

I picked it up and dropped it back in the trunk. The pink pyjama case slithered to one side so that I knew the lid wouldn't close. I bent and pushed it back. Hurry, Cinnamon. Hurry. The pink case rustled. There was something inside.

I stood, not wanting to look, knowing that I should. I slid my hand in and found nothing but emptiness and an edge of loose lining with something bulky underneath. A bundle of letters. I pulled them out.

The envelopes were long and a yellowed white. In the top left hand corner of each one was printed FERRERO'S FOR FISH. *His* letters to *her*. I knew it. And I knew, too, that I couldn't bear to read them now, and that maybe I'd never be able to. If I left them here I'd certainly never read them. I wouldn't open these trunks again.

I stood, hesitating. Then I slammed the trunk lid, snapped the locks and took a deep breath. The letters were still in my hand. I went into the bathroom and pushed the bundle to the back of the Rookwood linen closet under the stacks of black sheets and towels.

It was only then that I heard the doorbell. It rang and rang, the sound bouncing from the walls as if it had been ringing forever.

I ran downstairs. Please let it be Dad, home early. Or Paul, bringing the dog. Yes, Paul, please, or JoJo! Of course it would be JoJo. I'd told Paul to send him home. I flung the door open. There was no one there. But I saw the ghost car, waiting silently in front of the steps. It was better, now that I could see the outline. At least I knew where it was. But it was worse too. I knew for sure it was there. That strange black outline with the space where it should have been solid, that . . .

I heard my own little yelp of terror.

There was a driver now. He had no more substance than the car. I saw only the outside perimeter of the body and head, the featureless face turned in my direction, the cap . . . the cap with the peak.

Felix wouldn't be caught dead without his trusty yachting cap, I thought idiotically. *Anyone for sailing?*

Chapter 7

Cinnamon! Cinnamon!" It was JoJo's voice, and suddenly he appeared from the street behind the low wall. I was seeing him through the transparent car, and as he moved, I realized that I was seeing him, too, through the transparent body of Felix Ferrero.

"JoJo!" I whimpered. My hand fluttered in a silly effort to make him go around the outline of the car, not through it. But he was heading toward me by the quickest possible route.

There was a small girl with him, and they were carrying something big and heavy between them. It was a rumple of furry, squirming dog. JoJo had the feet and the girl had the top half.

JoJo was yelling at me. The dog struggled, yelping little frantic barks, the kind of sound I'd made myself when I got my first glimpse of the ghost driver in the ghost car.

"Where *were* you, Cinnamon?" JoJo yelled. "We

rang and rang, and then we went round the back, but it was locked and Jasper got away. Faddle, Jasper! Hold tight, Donna! We had to go all the way back to Donna's house almost and . . ."

The three of them were staggering right through the car. Belladonna's little figure blotted out Felix for a few seconds the way you'd blot out a slide on a screen by walking in front of the projector. I closed my eyes. This couldn't be happening! But how could I be imagining it all? There was too much!

As they came closer the tracing of the car and driver appeared again behind them. I saw Felix's hand come up and adjust the sailor's cap as if, somehow, it had been disturbed.

JoJo shouted at me from the bottom of the steps. "What are you *standing* there for, dumbo? Come and help us. Paul sent this dog for *you,* and me and Donna are having a real hard time with him."

I jerked my eyes from the waiting car.

"Hi," Donna gasped. "I'm Donna."

"Hi." I saw the terror in the dog's eyes just before it made one last, wild effort to free itself, leaped from their grasp and took off.

"Yipes!" JoJo said. "He scratched my arm off!"

I'd never seen a dog run like that, belly almost on the ground, big whisk of a tail drooping feebly behind it. I watched it go round the car in a wide, wide circle, all the time making little growling sounds in its throat.

"Is he having some kind of a fit or something?" JoJo asked.

"I don't know." Belladonna stood with her feet apart and her hands on her hips, watching the dog go.

"He *loves* to go places. Stupid dog doesn't know what he wants."

"Never mind," I said quickly. "Come on in. There's another can of apple juice." I glanced over my shoulder. The car was still there, but the dog had vanished. That dog wasn't stupid! It knew. At least that meant there was *something* there and I wasn't crazy. It did mean that, didn't it?

"I hope you haven't pigged out on those Fig Newtons, Cinnamon," JoJo warned. "If you have, you're in big trouble."

I got the three of us safe inside and locked the door.

Belladonna was looking up at me. She was about the same size as JoJo, but chunkier, with short, blond hair and the face of an angel. She pursed her lips and then said, "You're *real* tall. And you know what? You're even prettier than Alison. *We* thought *she* was some looker!"

In spite of the horror outside, I couldn't help smiling. She probably picked up on everything her two big brothers said.

"Some looker, huh?" I repeated.

"Yeah. But Donna thinks you're even better." JoJo stuck an elbow in Belladonna's ribs. "I told you my sister was a looker. And you should see her dance! Man, she's a looker then, all right!"

"Let's get the apple juice," I told them.

They raced ahead of me into the kitchen. So, she thought I was even prettier than Alison. Had Paul said that? At another time it might have mattered. Now I had other things to worry about.

JoJo climbed on the countertop to reach the glasses,

while Belladonna headed straight for the Fig Newtons on the table. She picked up the package and smiled at me, showing her little pearly teeth. "Is it all right if I take these out?"

"Sure," I said. "Help yourself."

"I'm not talking about the cookies," Donna said impatiently.

"Wait for me!" JoJo yelled. "Don't do it till I get down."

The minute he hit the ground Belladonna stuck a finger in her mouth and lifted out about half of her teeth.

"Smile!" JoJo urged.

She did. There were gaps everywhere.

"She looks just like the pumpkin we carved last year," JoJo said admiringly.

"Well! Goodness!" I told her. "You sure fooled me, Donna."

Belladonna slid the pink plastic with the teeth stuck in it on the counter. "Don't mess with this now, JoJo. Teeth are expensive."

"Ah . . . how come you have them?" I asked. It was wonderful to be with these two little kids. Life seemed almost normal. I felt protected by them. As long as I didn't think past now, or outside of this bright, safe kitchen.

"She got a bunch knocked out playing touch football," JoJo explained. "She does commercials. She's a *real* TV star!" It wasn't hard to see that JoJo was in love. "Do what you do on TV, Donna!"

Donna put her hands on her hips and spoke wearily. "Gee, Mom," she said. "How come my sweater doesn't feel soft the way it usually does? Did you forget to use the Soft As Silk? You know I love it when my sweaters have that silky soft feeling." She looked up at me. "I talk better when my flippers are out, but I look better when they're in," she explained.

"Oh."

"I can eat better without them too," she added.

The phone rang as she and JoJo wrestled over the Fig Newton package. I lifted it from its hook.

"This is Dr. Berringer returning your call," the voice said.

"Oh, hello." I glanced at JoJo and Belladonna.

"Can we go upstairs to play?" JoJo asked. "I want to show her my Mr. Robot. Can we take the cookies?"

Upstairs? Would the kids be safe? As safe as down here where they'd walked right through the ghost car.

"Just one second, Dr. Berringer." I covered the mouthpiece with my hand. "Stay away from that rose room, okay? The window's dangerous."

"Come on," JoJo yelled, leading the way.

I took my hand from over the phone. "Excuse me, Dr. Berringer. I had to speak to my little brother. It was good of you to call. You should have made it collect."

"That's all right. I recognized the phone number. You're at 220 Anderson Street in Sausalito. Right? Where we lived for a short time. Curiosity wouldn't let me *not* return a call like this. What can I do for you? I'm guessing you're another summer tenant and not a new owner."

"We're only here for three months." I searched for words. "I really wanted to speak to your daughter, Lisa. But I didn't know how to find her."

71

"Lisa?" I sensed the change in his voice in just that one word.

"I need to know some things about this house." Suddenly I remembered Alison asking if I were doing a school project. "I'm writing a paper about it," I said, glancing at my list of questions that still lay on the table and feeling that what I said wasn't really a lie. He was still silent.

"Lisa wasn't very happy there," he said at last. "It wasn't . . . a happy time for any of us."

"I understand." I did. If she'd seen and heard the things I'd seen and heard, I'd bet she wasn't too happy. But he wouldn't want to admit to stuff like that would he? It wouldn't make his daughter sound exactly normal. I knew about that too.

"I'm frightened," I said. "I need to talk to . . ."

His voice was sharp. "Look here, young lady—what was your name again—Cinnamon. My daughter's doing well now. I don't want her . . . disturbed. Whatever your problem, there must be someone else you can talk to. What does Lisa have to do with it?"

He wasn't going to tell me. And there *was* something to tell. I ran my finger along the same crack in the painted wall. It was a river, a river with little tributaries going nowhere. "Oh, please." I was whispering. "There isn't anybody else I *can* talk to. My mom and my sister died in an accident last year, and there's just my dad and my little brother. JoJo's too young to help and Dad, well, he . . ." I blinked away my tears. Why had I said that? Because I was desperate. And because all I'd told him was true.

I held the phone as if it were a lifeline and waited with my eyes tight shut. Something had definitely happened to Lisa in this house, and her father knew what it was.

"You are in a lonely spot, aren't you. Lisa, at least, had me." He cleared his throat. "Do you have a pencil?"

"Yes. Oh, thank you." I grabbed the one on the table and pulled the pad close.

"Lisa's actually living not far from you. She's at the Computer College on Mission Street in San Francisco, learning about hardware and software and something called bytes." He laughed a gruff laugh. "She's over everything. She came out okay."

I nodded, even though he couldn't see me. Lucky Lisa. "Her phone number is 555-3232." He waited, I guess so I could write it down, then added, "She's very happy right now."

It didn't sound like a warning. It was more of a plea to me not to make her unhappy again.

"Thank you," I said. "I promise I'll be very careful."

When I put the phone back I sat, looking at the number on the paper. I wrote LISA above it and drew circles around the name, circles and more circles. What would she tell me? Suppose her experiences *had* been the same as mine, well, that meant they really happened and neither one of us was crazy. Not Loony Lisa. Not Crazy Cinnamon. That would be something at least. I could take it to Dad then. I'd say, "Look, I don't want you to start worrying that I've gone wooly headed again. There's a ghost in this house, or rather outside this house. He's doing strange things to me. I know you can't see him and neither can JoJo, but he's there and I'm not imagining it because Lisa, the girl

73

who used to live here, saw him too. And I want to get out of here. I want us to start looking for somewhere else to live right now, because I can't take this one second longer."

Upstairs I could hear thumps and giggles and the creak, creak of Mr. Robot on the move. Thank heavens the kids were here in the house with me. I wished the dog were here too. But he wouldn't be. He'd never be.

I said Lisa's telephone number out loud as I dialed.

"Hello?"

"Hello. Is this Lisa?"

"Yes."

My heart was thumping so hard it hurt. "My name is Cinnamon Cameron. I'm staying in the house on Anderson Street, the Rookwood's? The place you stayed for a while last summer?"

I heard her draw in her breath, but she didn't speak.

"There's something wrong in this house," I said. "Isn't there?"

It almost seemed as if I could hear her heart beating in time with my own. "I talked to your father," I went on. "He was the one who gave me this number." And I'd promised him I'd be careful. I'm sorry, Dr. Berringer.

Lisa had a light, high voice that sounded like a little kid's. If I hadn't known better, I'd have thought she was JoJo's age. "What do you find wrong?" Fake casual. But she was using it on an expert.

"The same things you did," I said.

"My, that sounds ominous." Fake, tinkly laugh.

"Look," I asked. "Could I meet you? Could I come into San Francisco so we could talk?"

"Well, I don't mean to be rude, but I haven't any idea what we would talk about. And I'm very busy."

"We could talk about ghosts," I said. "A ghost car? Roses?"

The silence was a couple of heartbeats too long before she said shakily, "I think you're out of your mind."

There was a click, and the dial tone buzzed angrily in my ear.

"Lisa," I said. "Don't go. Wait! Lisa!" But she was gone. Slowly I put the phone back on its hook.

"Was that Loony Lisa you were talking to?"

I jumped and swung around.

Belladonna and JoJo were in the kitchen behind me. They'd slipped in, quiet as fish.

I stared aghast.

"Surprise!" JoJo shouted.

"How do you like us?" JoJo shouted.

"Oh, no," I moaned. "No!"

JoJo was wearing one of Dad's jackets and his Irish tweed hat. He'd penciled in a black mustache on his upper lip. And Belladonna! Belladonna was draped in the white dress that had been on the lid of the trunk. Emily's dress. She wobbled along on the white satin pumps, holding onto the side of the table with one hand, raising the full, fluffy skirt with the other. Two spots of red lipstick glowed on her cheeks and the beaded purse was tucked under one arm.

"No! No!" I said again. "Take those off. JoJo, you know you're not supposed . . ."

"Oh, Faddle, Cinnamon-Stick. Dad wouldn't mind. And those are just old things me and Donna found in a trunk. We got dressed up, that's all."

"Well, go upstairs right now and take them off. No, take them off here! Now." I was terrified. What if the ghost could see into the kitchen, could see this little toothless person in Emily's clothes?

"Now." My hands trembled as I lifted the hem of the dress and began tugging it over Belladonna's head.

"Yow!" she squeaked. "You're pulling my hair. Something's caught."

"Kick off the shoes." I snatched the purse from the table where she'd set it.

"Gee, Cinnamon. How come you're such an old grouch?" JoJo demanded.

I paid no attention. The dress was off. "Put this back in the trunk exactly the way you found it." I stopped. *I* had to put it back. It had to be just right. Nothing of Emily's must be disturbed. "I'll do it," I said. "And don't either of you, ever again, touch the things in those trunks. They don't belong to us."

I ran up the stairs, the dress folded across my arm, the shoes and the purse in my other hand. There was no time for terror. I had to do it.

I put everything on the tray, the way it had been before, with the dress spread on top. I smelled the mothball smell, and then, suddenly it was gone. In its place came the sweet, faint drift of roses. Something brushed my cheek and I felt all at once warm and loved and cherished. I put my hand to my face and smiled, then my eyes opened wide. What was I doing? Enjoying a ghost touch? Feeling less alone because of him? I must be crazy, all right.

"Get away," I said out loud. "I don't want your approval. Don't you try to get to me like this."

I slammed the lid of the trunk and ran as from a

thousand demons. Talking to myself! Or talking to a ghost! Either way didn't bear thinking about.

Belladonna and JoJo stood at the kitchen table examining my pad of paper.

I ran across and snatched it up. "You two!" I said. "You'd better learn that you don't get into other people's things, and you don't read what other people have written. Not unless you have permission."

"Oh, faddle, Cinnamon," JoJo said. "She thinks she's so *big*," he told Donna. "Ever since Mom died old Cinnamon thinks she's the boss and . . ." He stopped and darted a quick glance at me.

"Go wash off your mustache, JoJo," I said. "You could use a wash, too, Donna. Here, do it at the sink!"

Belladonna was looking at me with her round, blue eyes. "Was that Lisa's name you put all the circles around?"

"Yes."

"See? I told you, JoJo," she said smugly. She jerked a thumb at JoJo. *"He* said there had to be an *E* in Lisa." She looked up at me again. *"We* knew Lisa. She was . . ." Her fingers made circles at the side of her head. "She was *real* loony."

"Was she a kid or a person?" JoJo asked.

"Middle-aged, like her." Belladonna nodded toward me. "Lisa told me a poem once. She said she made it up. But I'm not allowed to say it."

"Is it nasty?" JoJo asked.

"No."

"How come you're not allowed to say it, then?"

"Because it gave me bad dreams." Belladonna picked up her flippers, slid them in and jiggled her face to make them fit right.

"You can tell us," JoJo wheedled.

"Stop bugging her, JoJo. If she's not allowed to tell, she shouldn't," I said.

"Well, here it is," Belladonna said in a rush. "I'll tell if you want." She closed her eyes tight and spoke so fast that the words blurred. But I heard every one of them.

> Ghost before me,
> Ghost behind me,
> No place to hide,
> Ghost will find me.

JoJo moved a step closer to me. "That's scary all right."

"It's just silly," I said. "Go wash your face, JoJo."

Chapter 8

That night I dreamed I was dancing again, floating across the stage, my feet in my worn satin toe shoes scarcely touching the boards.

"Colette wants to see you," someone yelled. "In her office."

"I won't go. She just wants to tell me that Mom and Marissa are dead."

"No, she doesn't. They're not dead. It's all a mistake."

"A mistake?" Oh, the joy. The sudden, sweet soaring joy as I wakened. Mother wasn't dead! But she was. The coldness rushed in. It was always so cruel to waken from that dream. I must have had it a hundred times, sleeping and waking, since the plane crash. Misery washed over me again, fresh and new as it had been on that awful day.

I lay shivering.

"Colette wants to see you."

I'd been rehearsing the Pas de Paysan from "Giselle."

"I think that it will be a perfection for you to be the young peasant girl," Colette had said, nodding her little bird head. "You have all of the energy, *ma chérie*. The *joie de vivre*."

I'd almost stopped breathing. I knew that Cynthia Gregory, almost the top ballerina in all of America, was to dance the part of Giselle. To be on the same stage, on the same program with Cynthia Gregory! I would miss out on the trip to Rome, but so what? This was dancing, and dancing was my life. I gave my ticket to Marissa. It was a charter flight, and there was no way to turn it in.

"But are you sure, Cinnamon-Pie?" Marissa stared at me with big, shining eyes. "*You* were the one who wanted to go so badly. *You* were the one who talked Mom into it. You're certain, absolutely, never-to-be-sorry-certain? Because if you say you aren't, I think I'll just die."

I lay in bed now, scrunching myself up, remembering. Marissa *had* died, and so had Mom. There was no mistake. Moonlight came white through the rows of windows to lie across the floor. The bedroom door was closed. Since I came back from the hospital, I always slept with my door open. I'd had enough of being shut in, shut up, shut away. But here, in the ghost house, I closed anything I could close. Oh, Mom, protect me. Look after me the way you always did.

I'd asked Dad if we could put a lock high on the door of the rose room to keep JoJo out.

"I'll buy one and put it on at the weekend," Dad said.

Maybe a lock would keep Felix away from the rest of the house, I thought. Away from me.

80

No, no. Think about good things now. Don't let *him* into your head again.

Dad had looked so happy when he came home tonight.

"The job's going well." He'd smiled one of his old familiar crinkly smiles that I'd missed these past months. "All my choo-choos ran on schedule."

"That's great, Dad." I'd realized that the lines down his cheeks were smoothing out.

Tomorrow I'd spend the whole day with Paul. There'd be just the two of us. How would it be? I thought about Paul's brown arms, and the way his hands were, thin and strong. I thought about him shirtless in the market and the way he'd held me close in the rose room. He had a really nice mouth. Would he ever kiss me? I pulled the covers closer around me. He was nice to think about all right. Marissa would have liked him. "What a panda bear," she'd have said. "A perfect panda!" To be a perfect panda was Marissa's greatest compliment.

Best not to think any more about Marissa either.

Where would we go tomorrow, Paul and I? What would we do? I had to see Lisa. If I asked Paul to take me to the Computer College, he would. But I didn't want him there when I confronted Lisa about the ghost poem, and why she'd gone so suddenly from the Rookwood house. The day after tomorrow I'd try to find the college myself, and I'd find her too. Part of the mystery lay with her. So Paul and I would be alone. I held that thought close, as close as I held the hairbrush as I went to sleep.

* * *

There was fog again in the early morning, rolling in from the bay to fill the spaces between the hills, hiding everything beyond the walls of the old house.

Oh, no, I thought. I peered out of the kitchen window. What would happen to our day now? Would Paul still want to go?

As soon as Dad left for work, I started to fix the picnic lunch. I'd act as if we were still going, and then we would. It would be like a magic charm. I made big, chunky cheese sandwiches on wheat bread, washed apples and made enough hot chocolate to fill the Thermos.

JoJo was watching Mr. Rogers on TV and slurping up granola. "I'm glad I'm going to Donna's," he told me. "She's going to let me try her teeth flippers today." He looked up at me happily. "She says she only lets her very most special friends wear her flippers. That's because they're so expensive and because you don't want just anybody's spit getting all over *your* spit and . . ."

"I guess not," I said, fast, before he could go into any more detail.

It was exactly nine when the doorbell rang. JoJo and I ran together to open it, and there was Paul. He was wearing jeans, and the collar of the pale blue jacket he'd had on the first time I saw him was turned up against the morning cold. His hair sparkled, beaded with fog.

The woman with him was definitely his mother. She had a round, smiling face, just like Donna's, and long, brown-gray hair that was tied back in a pony tail. Underneath her open raincoat I could see a blue sweatshirt and jeans, both smeared with dried white paint.

"Hi, Paul," JoJo said. "Hi, Mrs. Russell."

Mrs. Russell smiled. "Hi, yourself." She held out a yellow bowl filled with strawberries. "These are for you, Cinnamon. They're fresh from the garden. Paul said he'd bring them over, but I wanted to come."

"Oh, thank you." I stepped aside. "Please. Come in." I glanced quickly into the driveway before I closed the door behind them, but if the ghost car was there, I couldn't see it through the fog.

"I'm really sorry I didn't come sooner to welcome you. But I've been painting." Mrs. Russell swung her coat open, made a face and closed it again quickly. "I don't mean the Van Gogh kind of painting either. I'm talking about walls and ceilings."

"Oh." I glanced quickly at Paul. "I don't know if we're still going somewhere or not. But if you're painting, I'm sure you don't want JoJo," I began.

Mrs. Russell interrupted. "Of course I want JoJo. He and I are buddies. In fact Donna and JoJo are going to help me paint today."

"Oh, boy! We are?" JoJo asked.

I opened my eyes wide.

Paul smiled. "Mom's brave. It comes from teaching second grade. And what do you mean, you don't know if we're going somewhere? If we stopped what we were doing up here every time we have fog or rain or mist—we'd be hermits. Besides, it'll clear. You'll see. Or else we'll drive out of it."

"So why don't JoJo and I just go now?" Mrs. Russell put an arm around JoJo's shoulders. "And don't worry about his clothes getting messed up, Cinnamon. I have some of the boys' old shirts for them to wear."

"Thanks for having him," I said.

I heard JoJo talking all the way through the hall. "Can me and Donna do the ceilings?" I heard the front door click closed behind them.

"Well," I said, suddenly a little shy. Dumb to be shy. But I was remembering the way I'd thought about Paul last night in bed, thinking about him kissing me, and stuff like that. "The picnic's ready." I sounded as breathless as if I'd run three miles.

"Great. So let's get going. Oh, first I want to tell you about Jasper. I was planning on bringing him? Belladonna said he wouldn't stay yesterday, so I thought we'd take him with us today so he'd get to know you. The dog's gone wacko. He came out with Mom and me, tail wagging, the works. And I thought it was going to be okay. But as soon as we started over here, he took off. Man, I didn't know that old mutt could run that fast! He's high in the hills by now. You know, he only did that once before. It was when Lisa was here. He stayed away for days."

I swallowed. Smart old dog. "It doesn't matter," I said. "The food's on the kitchen table if you want to grab it. I'll get a coat."

I ran upstairs, past the rose room, and took my jacket from the bedroom closet. I brushed my hair quickly in front of the mirror and put on some lipstick. Donna had said I was prettier than Alison. Well, no need to feel so good about that. What did a six-year-old kid know anyway? I leaned closer to the mirror and smoothed a finger over my cheekbones. Did Paul think I was pretty? I guess some of the guys did, back home. But they'd backed off fast when I freaked out. So don't do *that* again, I advised myself. Be like everyone else. Be happy and fun to be with. Keep out the bad thoughts.

I ran back down the stairs.

The front door lay open. I wished Paul hadn't left it like that. Anything could have come in. I glanced nervously around the hall. It was still and quiet, watching me with its empty eyes. It's not watching you! Stop that, Cinnamon. Just stop it!

Paul's voice floated in from outside. "I've got everything, Cinnamon. Ready when you are."

I checked that I had the key and shut the house door behind me.

Paul had his headlights on, and he'd left the door on the passenger side open. I ran across and slid in. No other lights reflected in the rearview mirror. No other motor started when Paul turned on ours. I made myself sit back and tried to relax. We were on our way.

Mrs. Russell's car was a big, well-used station wagon. There were magazines and loose papers around my feet, and when I looked in back, I saw old paint cans and a paper sack with wallpaper rolls sticking out of it.

Paul glanced back too. "She's planning on papering the bathroom next. Mom always has a project going."

"My mom was like that too."

Paul eased the car out of the driveway. I told myself I wouldn't look behind to see if we were being followed, but the urge was too strong. I saw only the side of the house, its brown shingles wet and shining. Nothing but fog closed in behind us. Ghost behind me?

Maybe not. Maybe he'd taken the day off. Or maybe he didn't know I'd be out and moving so early.

"Mrs. Cram's not home yet," Paul said, nodding toward the cottage, half hidden by the fog at the first dip in the hill.

"She's gone somewhere?"

"Yep. She goes to visit her daughter a lot of the time. We always know when she gets back. Smoke comes out of her chimney. That fireplace is the only heating she has. We kid her about it. It's like when the Queen's in residence at Buckingham Palace, they run up the flag? When Nellie Cram's in residence, she runs up her smoke."

I sat quietly. Too bad she was gone. I wanted to talk to her so badly. I'd just have to watch for the smoke signal too.

The station wagon swung right at the bottom of the hill. Paul grinned at me. "You know what people around here call Anderson Street? The funnel! The fog just seems to ooze up from the bay. It'll be better when we get across the bridge."

We were climbing now through a grayness that billowed around us, soft as clouds. On either side were the misty green hills of Marin. In a few minutes we were on the Golden Gate, crossing high above the bay. Fog hung in tatters around the rust red uprights of the bridge, drifting under us and above. Cars sizzled past, their headlights splintering the gloom. Below on the invisible bay, foghorns moaned.

"Sorry about this," Paul said.

I was sorry too. But the fog had its compensations. It was snug in the warm, friendly old station wagon.

Ghost will find me? Not here, surely. I felt safe.

The city loomed ahead, misty and obscure. I saw tall white skyscrapers pushing together, the bay lapping at their feet. Traffic lights shimmered red and yellow and green and there seemed to be a million people on the sidewalks. Like back home, I thought, but somehow different. The streets seemed to all go straight up and straight down, and the houses were joined together higgledy-piggledy, houses of all colors with big high windows to catch the views of bay and bridges. Cable cars rattled out of the fog banks, clanging and wheezing, and then suddenly I saw that we were heading straight down on a street that led to the water, and that the fog had disappeared.

"Look up, Cinnamon!" Paul said. "Didn't I tell you we'd have sunshine?"

I looked out of the window past his head, and saw that the sky was turning blue, and then, magically, the sun peeked out lighting up the whole, gray world.

"Okay?" Paul asked.

"Very okay," I said.

Paul parked the station wagon in a lot whose sign said WELCOME TO FISHERMAN'S WHARF and we walked on old, cracked sidewalks through fish and tar smells, past stalls mounded with lobsters, past chowder bubbling in great earthenware vats. There was a big, black sailing ship tied at the dock, its masts reaching for the sky, its rigging spread like a giant spiderweb against the clouds. There were flower shops with pots of tousle-headed chrysanthemums lined up outside. There was a clown blowing balloons. It was even warm.

Paul took off his blue jacket and smiled down at me. "In San Francisco we get summer and winter in one day. Like it?"

"I love it."

He put a quarter in a telescope so I could look at Alcatraz lying bare and ugly in the middle of the bay, and his arm was around my shoulders while I looked, and his head was close to mine. I could smell a spicy, fresh cologne. There was a feeling inside me of being tingly and alive. And happy. Later he left me for a second while he went into a small shop and bought me a yellow cap with I LEFT MY HEART IN SAN FRANCISCO written on it. It had a peak, and for a minute I thought of Felix, about the way he wouldn't be caught dead without his yachting cap, and I wished Paul had bought something else for me instead. But I forgot about Felix when Paul put the cap on my head. He pushed my hair back, and his golden eyes smiled into mine.

"Pretty!" he said.

I felt my cheeks burn. Did he mean me? Or my hair? Or the dumb cap?

He took my hand in his and held it while we walked. After a while we leaned on the railing looking across the bay, his hand still warm around mine. A pigeon strutted along the top board in front of us, and I stepped back to let it through. I watched it swagger away, its tail feathers bouncing, and as I turned I saw Felix.

He leaned across the railing, too, not looking at us. How long had he been there? Oh, God! He was a cartoon drawing, unfinished, his traced-out hands folded in front of him on the solid wood, the peak of the yachting cap pulled down over eyes that weren't there.

"No," I whispered.

"No, what?" Paul was looking down at me. "I didn't ask you anything. Did you think I did?"

"Can we go now, Paul? Isn't there something else you want to show me? You said . . ." I couldn't think what he'd said.

Felix had turned toward us, his faceless face watching.

"Sure." I sensed Paul's puzzlement. "You want to head for the beach?"

"Yes. But, ssh! Don't talk so loud." Paul was staring at me. I lowered my own voice to a whisper in case Felix could hear. Senseless. He could probably hear the thoughts darting around inside my head. "Yes," I said. "The beach. You want to run?" I asked, desperately. "Let's run."

"Sure."

We raced together along the wharf, scattering pigeons and doves, past the wax museum, past a mime who smiled at us as we streaked past. Were there ghost feet pounding behind us? I couldn't hear for the pounding of my heart.

Breathless, we collapsed in the station wagon.

"Go! Go!" I urged.

"You really like things to move fast, don't you," Paul teased. He laughed down at me, then leaned across to hug me. His face was cold against mine, and his hair was ruffled. I wanted to hug him back, but I was frozen. He moved away a little and adjusted my cap. "There," he said, and I could tell he was embarrassed. Face it, most girls would have hugged him back, all right. Maybe he thought I didn't want to? I managed a smile.

I sat stiffly on the edge of the seat as we eased out of the parking lot and up the hill. Where was the ghost car? Felix could have left it anywhere. In the middle of the street even. There couldn't be rules for ghost cars. I stared unseeing through the window.

"That's Coit Tower, up there," Paul said and I tried to look interested. We were passing the painted houses again. A mosque with a golden dome slid past. I saw a priest in a long black robe, holding his black pie-shaped hat against the wind. And I saw the ocean again, or maybe the bay.

"That's Seal Rock out there," Paul said. "And those are seals. We're coming up to Ocean Beach."

It was ocean indeed. Great, green waves rolled in to shore, and the sea tossed angrily, striped with ribbons of foam.

"This isn't my beach though," Paul said, and we were driving on.

I looked back once and saw nothing. But I wasn't fooled this time. He was there. Somewhere. Ghost behind me. Ghost will find me. I slid lower in my seat.

"You don't talk much, do you?" Paul asked.

"I'm sorry."

"Don't be. It's nice to be quiet."

There were green hills ahead now and the sky kept changing, clouds coming and going, moving like dancers across a stage. I would have loved it—if things had been different.

It was about a half hour before Paul pulled the car over and parked on the side of the road. There were

90

thick growing bushes and I couldn't see the ocean, but I could hear it somewhere below.

"We're here," Paul said. "My own private beach."

He opened the door and a fresh sea wind rushed into the car.

"Brrr," he said. "Button up. It's going to be cold."

"But nice," I added. *Oh, if only it would be nice.*

"It's too early to eat, isn't it?" Paul asked. "Let's walk first, and I'll come back for the food."

Traffic zoomed by us as we stepped out of the car, and even though I'd told myself not to hope, I couldn't help it. Maybe we *had* lost him this time. Please. Please.

We went down a narrow, dirt path, Paul ahead, stopping me when I slipped, the wind pulling his blue jacket tight across his shoulders. But he didn't take my hand, and I knew things were different between us. Maybe it was because I'd been unfriendly when he'd hugged me in the car. Or maybe he was beginning to sense my craziness and wanted no part of it. Just the way it had happened with the other guys back home. *But I'm not crazy. Susan Shrink says I'm not and she knows.*

It was a wild empty beach that lay at the bottom of the cliff. It matched my mood. Gulls huddled in a clump, facing the moving sea, their feathers ruffled by the wind. Farther up, high above the tide line, a man sat with his back to us, tending a bright crackling fire.

My heart was hammering again. Was it Felix, here before us? No. This figure was bulky. He wore a black windbreaker, and as his face turned briefly in our direction, I saw the flow of a dark beard. No cap—no peak that would warn me of ghosts.

Paul and I walked in the other direction. "There's never been anyone here before," he said. I noticed how he kept his hands deep in the pockets of the blue windbreaker and how he left a small space between us. *Oh, Paul!*

Sand blew in little spatters against the bottoms of our jeans, and it was so fine that our feet sank into it, like into fresh snow. Way out on the green, foam-flecked ocean a sailboat strained, dipping before the wind, the same wind that tugged at my cap, almost pulling it from my head. I grabbed for it, and at the same time I sensed a movement behind us. For a second I thought it was the man with the beard. But it wasn't.

It was Felix.

He walked as we walked. I saw the scuff of our footprints in the sand, and his overlapping them, his feet as big as Paul's feet, his stride as long

I heard myself sob. The wind carried the sound away.

Paul kicked at a pile of black seaweed. "Kelp," he said. "It comes in when there's a storm."

I didn't answer. My eyes were on Felix who had stopped when we stopped. I'd never been this close to him. It was so frightening that I wanted to run, into the sea, anywhere. How could a person be entirely flat and one-dimensional and still move? How could he see with no eyes and hear with no ears? Maybe he worked on radar, like a bat.

This time, when I made some sort of sound, Paul heard.

"What is it, Cinnamon? Can't you tell me?"

What if I said, "Look. Look at the ghost"? Oh, that would be the end of everything, all right. But he *must* be able to see Felix. He was only a few paces away.

My hand shook as I raised it and pointed. "What's that, Paul?"

I saw the puzzlement in his face. "What's what? Oh, you mean that concrete thing sticking into the sea? It's part of an old jetty."

The footprints? I pointed down. "I mean those tracks. The ones beside ours."

"I don't see any, Cinnamon. There's no one here but us and that guy at the fire." He bent closer to the sand, then straightened. "You really look cold, Cinnamon. I probably shouldn't have brought you here."

"Oh, you should. You should. I love it." I was talking too loudly. Felix turned to stare seaward.

"Why don't you go up by the fire?" Paul asked. He looked cold too. Cold and very far away. "I'll get the Thermos."

I watched him walk slowly away, his head down, his hands deep in his pockets, and I was hurting inside. However hard I tried to be like everyone else, I wasn't.

"Because you're crazy, that's why," a horrible voice inside me whispered.

"No, I'm not," I said out loud. "I'm not."

And then I was running again, toward the fire, away from Felix, away from myself.

I could smell woodsmoke on the wind, and it made me cough as I came to a stop on the other side of the fire from the man with the beard.

He smiled up at me. His teeth glimmered white

through his beard and he said, "Hi, why don't you stand over here. Upwind. It's more comfortable. And I'll be able to see you."

"I'm Cinnamon." I pushed my hair back under my cap and moved beside him. He was younger than I'd thought at a distance, and he had a look of strength that came from his size. He was enormous, a great bull of a man.

"Is it okay if I share your fire for a few minutes?"

"Do that." His voice was deep like a gong, and then I saw that he was peering through the smoke.

"What about your friend?" he asked. "Wouldn't he like to get warm too?"

I thought he meant Paul, but as I turned I saw that Paul was halfway up the path, and that the man was looking straight at the ghost of Felix Ferrero.

Chapter 9

This stranger could see the ghost too! Relief sang inside me. I'd had a lot of fears since we moved into the old Rookwood house. But I knew now that my biggest fear was not of the ghost. It was that there *was* no ghost.

The man prodded at the fire and smoke belched around us. I choked the words out somehow.

"You can see him too."

"See who?"

"The ghost. You said . . ."

He held up his hand. "Just a minute now. I said nothing about any ghost." It might have been the smoke that made his eyes narrow, but I didn't think so.

"You were *looking* at him. You said, 'What about your friend . . .' "

"Wasn't there a friend with you?"

I nodded. "Yes. Paul. But you saw someone else,

95

didn't you? After Paul left? Please, please tell me that you did."

The man threw another piece of driftwood on the fire so the flames dimmed for a minute, then burst high in a crackle of sparks.

"There *was* someone else on the beach a while back. I thought he came with you, but he might not have. I don't see anybody now."

I stepped to the side of the smoke. The beach lay empty. A gray pelican glided silently overhead and the gulls stood clumped together against the wind. Felix had gone. And then I saw Paul coming down the path from the road, the blue Thermos cradled in his arms. I wanted to throw myself down by the fire and bawl. For a minute I'd thought I'd found someone who saw what I saw. I'd thought I could tell Paul, "There's a ghost in the Rookwood house. He's following me. He followed me here today." And the man would nod and say, "No kidding. He's really there. She isn't crazy." But it wasn't going to be that easy.

Paul was sprinting toward us.

"What did he look like?" I asked quickly. "The third person? At least tell me that."

The man shrugged. "He wasn't that close, and I wasn't paying much attention."

"Was he wearing a jacket? A cap?"

"I didn't notice." The man waved the smoke away from the front of his face with short, angry chops of his hand. "If I did see someone, believe me, he was no ghost. There's no such thing. No, of course not."

I could tell he was angry, but I didn't know why. When someone suggests you've seen a ghost you might be scared or embarrassed. You might even laugh and say, "What are you—kooky or something?" But why be angry?

Paul came round the side of the fire. He had two paper cups along with the Thermos. "Hi. How are you doing now, Cinnamon?" He held out his hand to the man with the beard. "I'm Paul Russell. I guess you already met Cinnamon. We've got three cups. Who'd like some hot chocolate?"

"I would, for one." The man shook Paul's outstretched hand. "Amos Piper."

Paul seemed to hesitate. Then he smiled and said, "Hi. Nice fire you've got."

The man stared at him for a second and then back into the flames. His name had meant something to Paul, and it meant something to me too. It was a name I'd heard before, but I couldn't remember where.

Amos Piper crouched over the fire, and Paul and I stood, all three of us sipping without talking. A gust of wind carried the smoke away in a cloud, and for a minute I could see the beach beyond. No Felix. Where had he gone? I looked behind me. Nothing but the blowing sand and the cliff of scrub and dirt that rose to the highway. He'd gone, but it was too late for me. He'd been around long enough to spoil the day and whatever had been nice between Paul and me. Maybe that was what he'd intended to do.

The man's voice startled me. He was speaking to Paul, softly, almost dreamily.

"You know who I am, don't you?"

"Maybe."

"You know." He pitched his styrofoam cup into the fire where it sizzled and clung to the burning wood, melting like rubber.

"It wasn't my fault, you know," he said, still in that faraway voice. "The newspapers called me the Pied Piper, but that wasn't fair. I didn't lead them. The thrust was mine, but they followed freely. I only told them the truth."

"I'm sure you did." Paul was tugging at my arm. "It's time we were heading for home. Come on, Cinnamon."

As I moved I sensed something on the other side of the fire, a fleeting shape that was clear for only a moment before it was swallowed up again in the smoke. Felix! But I'd seen more than that at that first flicker of movement. The man's head had turned, too, in Felix's direction. He'd seen what I'd seen and at the same time.

I shook Paul's hand away. "Wait a second. Mr. Piper? Is there someone else here? Someone besides us?"

His smile gleamed through the beard. "God, maybe. They tell me he's everywhere. I saw him once, in a wave."

"Come on, Cinnamon." Paul's arm was around my shoulders and his voice was urgent. "It's getting late. You're shivering again. Let's go."

The cup shook in my hand, hot chocolate slopping over the edge. He *had* seen. He *had*.

Amos Piper stood. He was an even bigger bear than I'd imagined, massive in his black jacket and pants, his feet enormous in laced boots. Massive chest. Massive voice that suddenly boomed around us.

"We are all one," he said. "If you want peace I will tell you where to find it." The massive arm lifted. "It's there, beyond the horizon. You want love? You must search it out. It hides at the place between sea and sky. We will go together."

Paul had backed away from the fire, pulling me with him, and now we were running, pounding along the beach with the man's voice still crashing behind us like the surf on the sand. "Not my fault. None of it. None. None."

I glanced over my shoulder when we were part way up the cliff path. He was standing with his head thrown back, sparks drifting around him.

And Felix? Felix was walking slowly at the ocean's edge.

"Come on"—Paul trailed me behind him—"I swear, sooner or later every crazy ends up in California. Can you believe walking onto that beach and right into the Pied Piper? And I let you go alone to that fire. I must be nutty myself. I'm sorry, Cinnamon."

"You couldn't help it. Wait." I stopped again to catch my breath. Strands of my hair blew across my face, and I bundled them back under the cap. Whoever that man was, he had seen Felix. That was something for me to hold on to. Maybe he was crazy. Maybe we both were. But surely two crazies wouldn't have exactly the same hallucination at exactly the same time?

I watched Felix now. He had turned his back on us and was staring across the ocean. What was he thinking? Did ghosts think? Where had he disappeared to, earlier? Maybe he went to the bathroom. Did ghosts do that?

We scrambled up the last few yards to the highway and Paul unlocked the car. This time I didn't try to make him hurry. I was learning that there was no way to outrun Felix. I was beginning to accept that wherever I was, he'd be there too.

Paul glanced at me as he eased the car into the traffic.

"So much for our picnic on the beach," he said.

So much for everything, I thought.

"Who is he, Paul? I knew I'd seen him somewhere before. He has to be some kind of cult leader."

"The Pied Piper. Don't you remember? He started a commune in Oregon. It ended up that his group took over the whole little town. It ended up worse than that."

Suddenly I did remember. "All those people died. His picture was on television, everywhere."

"I guess he's right when he says it wasn't his fault. At least, the courts agreed with him. They said it was mass hysteria. Someone started it, and they all followed, swimming out into the ocean."

I scrunched down in my seat. "Beyond the horizon," I said. "Between sea and sky. Looking for all those things. He didn't go with the others?"

"Oh, yes. But he had the strength to get back when he changed his mind. Some of his followers did too. But thirty or forty didn't make it. Weeks after, their bodies kept getting washed ashore." Paul was quiet for a minute. "He knows he's guilty as hell though. That's why he keeps saying over and over that he isn't. Denying like that is a dead giveaway."

Not always, I thought. I never denied. I accepted the blame right from the start.

Paul lifted a hand from the steering wheel and touched my arm. "You're still shivering, Cinnamon.

100

Are you okay? Geez, I'm sorry that had to happen. I'll stop at the first coffee shop we come to."

"I'm okay." I closed my eyes and pulled my jacket tight around me. Ghosts! The Pied Piper's life must be filled with them. Or else he was scared that it could be. Let one in, let them all in. No wonder he'd denied seeing Felix. Felix could have been one of *his*. But how could the Piper and *I* see him when Paul didn't? Or JoJo? Or Dad?

I put my hands across my lips, terrified at the answer that flashed into my mind. The Piper and I had killed! That put us on another plane. That made us approachable.

"Oh, no," I whispered.

Paul turned briefly toward me. "Hold on, Cinnamon. I know it was horrible. God! You're so pale." The car slowed. "Here's a turn-off. No coffee shop, but . . ."

The car's signal light blinked and went click-click-click on the dash, and then we were off the road and in some sort of rest area. Trees grew thickly on our right. Traffic whizzed by on the other side.

Paul cut the motor. He leaned toward me and took off my cap, smoothing my hair. His hands were cold as they moved down to my face. The front seat was all of a piece, and he slid across, close to me.

"Poor Cinnamon. And I wanted this to be such a terrific day."

"It's okay," I said again. My lips were stiff. I felt and sounded like some kind of robot. Piper and I, both of us empty spaces where ghosts could come.

Paul put his cheek against mine. I smelled again the spicy, cologne smell of his skin.

101

"The thing is, I can't tell what you're thinking. Ever. You get this strange, frightened kind of look, and it's as if you don't know I'm here. I'm not trying to bug you now. It's just that . . ."

"No!" I pushed him away. "Why are you doing this to me?" I heard my voice rising, and I half saw the shocked look on Paul's face and half knew that he thought I was talking to him. But I wasn't. "Get away," I screamed.

Felix Ferrero sat in the back of the station wagon, right next to the rolls of wallpaper. His feet were propped up on one of the cans of paint, and his cap was pulled down over his eyes, as if he were sleeping. Maybe he was. Maybe he was dead.

I thumped my fists against the back of the car seat. "Just get away and leave me alone. I can't stand any more."

"I'm sorry," Paul said stiffly. "Just forget it, okay?"

"Oh, Paul. I don't mean you."

"You don't, huh?" Paul slid back to his own side of the car.

"No. No. It's Felix. He's back there."

Paul glanced quickly into the back. "Sure. And that's who you're talking to."

I put my head down and covered my face with my hands. There was no use trying to explain. "I swear, sooner or later every crazy ends up in California," Paul had said. He was probably right. And it was all hopeless anyway.

Chapter 10

Paul came with me into the house. He unpacked the sandwiches I'd made, put them on a plate and set them on the table. He poured a glass of milk and left it on the table too.

"You might feel better if you eat," he said. They were the first words he'd spoken since we'd driven from the turn-off, when he'd tried to hold me and I'd pushed him away.

"There's enough for two," I said timidly.

"No, thanks, Cinnamon. I'll just go home."

I heard the front door slam behind him, and I was alone.

Unless Felix was here.

I let my eyes dart around the kitchen. No, he usually let me see his shadowy outline and—Oh, no. No! No!

I held onto the edge of the table, remembering. Today . . . he'd been more than an outline. He'd been solid, bulky, sitting there in the back of Paul's car with his feet on the can of paint and his hands in his pockets. He'd been like a person. He was filled in.

The refrigerator hummed busily. The wall clock ticked. I understood suddenly what Felix was doing. Little by little he was showing himself to me. First there'd been only the sound of his car, then its outline, then his. There would have been a face today, if I'd been able to see it under the tilted cap.

I heard myself moan. Now I had *that* to freak me out. What would it be like? A dead face? A skeleton head, like the awful things in horror movies?

I sat, afraid to move.

After a while JoJo came home.

"Hey, Cinnamon! How come you're back so quick? Me and Donna were painting horses all over the wall, and Mrs. Russell didn't mind as long as they were white horses 'cause that's what the wall's going to be tomorrow, and then Paul came in, and he was slamming doors and everything, and then Donna went, 'Uh-oh! Somebody's in a temper.' And she meant Paul. And then she went, 'Your sister probably wouldn't make out with him.' And she meant you, Cinnamon. And then her Mom went, 'That's enough, Donna.' And Donna made a face, like this . . .'" JoJo took time out to show me. "And then her mom was *really* mad and she said, 'No video games for you tonight, my girl.' And she meant Donna. And then she went off to talk to Paul. And then she came back and said I'd better go home." He stopped for breath. "So how come you're back so quick, Cinnamon?"

"No reason."

"Oh." He ate the sandwiches.

I patted the chair beside mine. "Come sit here,

JoJo." It was so wonderful not to be alone. I squeezed his hand.

"Quit that," JoJo said.

When Dad came home, I fixed eggs, and I told him I was sorry that was all there was and that I didn't feel very good.

I shouldn't have said that. But I was tired of pretending, and I felt awful.

It was only eight o'clock when I went to bed. I lay there trying to sort things out. There was some small relief that the ghost was a reality and not some strange happening inside my head. Thinking I was weirding out again was one kind of terror. But knowing that he was real and that he was haunting me was terror of another kind.

It all started with this house, I thought. If I can get away from here . . . but where? There was nowhere to go and no one to go to. I had to tell Dad. He was the only one I could turn to.

At nine he brought up honey and milk, the way Mom used to when one of us was sick and that made me cry.

"Oh, sweetie," he comforted, stroking my shoulder. Poor Dad.

He stayed while I drank, while my mind raced around, trying to find the best way to tell him.

"Dad?" I put the empty cup on the bedside table. "I know you've paid three months rent on this house and we can't afford just to lose all that money. But could we look for somewhere else? I . . . hate it here. I'm frightened. I can find a summer job and help financially. Please. Please. I just need to get away from here." I took Mom's silver hairbrush from under my pillow and held it against me the way a monk would hold a cross. "This place . . . it's making me sick again."

There it was. The weapon I'd thought I'd never use. But the one most certain to get results.

I saw the stricken look on Dad's face, the fear, and I couldn't believe I was doing this to him.

"You don't know everything," I went on, speaking quickly now, desperately. "There's a ghost here. His name is Felix Ferrero and he follows me everywhere I go."

Dad stood back, staring down at me. "Sweetie! Oh, sweetie!"

"He might even be here now, Dad. In this room. But I don't think so. At first he wasn't solid, but then little by little he filled in. He has a car, but you wouldn't be able to see it. I'm the only one. Well, maybe the Pied Piper could see it too."

Dad knelt by the bed, his arms around me. "There, there. It's going to be all right."

I wanted to push him away. That was a voice and a tone I knew. He was soothing me, humoring me. He didn't believe about the ghost. But he did believe I was getting sick again. That he believed, all right. I held on to him, digging my fingers into his arms. How could I blame him? Nobody would take this kind of stuff seriously. Hopeless, hopeless, hopeless.

"Poor little Cinnamon," Dad said. "You should have told me before about this ghost. I'm going to start looking for somewhere else tomorrow, first thing. I promise."

He hugged me tight, and I hugged him back, and then I lay down and turned my face to the wall. *Poor little Cinnamon* was right. And poor Dad too. But maybe we *could* find another place to live, and once we got away I'd make it all up to him. I'd be so nice and normal and healthy he'd never have to worry about me again.

Oh, really? I wished I wasn't the kind of person who could see every side of everything. Did I think I'd ever be nice and healthy and normal? Would I forget Felix Ferrero? And the Pied Piper? And my own terrible, awful guilt?

I'd be getting away from Paul too. I buried my face in the pillow, remembering the way he'd felt, the smell of his skin. "Pretty," he'd said, his voice whisper soft, his eyes filled with golden light. But then the coldness had come. "No, thanks, Cinnamon. I think I'll just go home."

No use worrying about Paul. Paul was gone from me already. And soon, soon Alison would be coming back to him. Alison who was nice and normal and healthy without even trying. So I'd worry instead about what *I* could do. I could try to find out everything I could about Felix Ferrero. I could read the letters. *No. No. No letters.* The thought of them made my heart pound. *Okay then, Cinnamon. Keep thinking.* There were things I knew. He was a ghost, therefore he was dead.

Tomorrow for sure, I'd go and see Lisa. If I had the San Francisco map, I could find out right away where Mission Street was and how to get there. That would be a start.

I got up quietly. Dad wasn't in bed yet and I didn't want him to see me when he thought he had me safely asleep.

I went quickly past the door of the rose room and down the wide staircase. The wood was cold and gritty under my feet. I remembered how I'd planned on polishing this staircase and making it beautiful. But that was when we first came. That was before.

Below me the hallway lay in darkness and outside there was more darkness, crowding against the walls, waiting to come in. The map was in the living room on top of the bookcase. There'd be no problem keeping out of Dad's way. He'd be in the kitchen still with his work spread across the table.

I paused halfway across the hall.

Dad was talking to someone. But wasn't JoJo in bed?

It took a couple of seconds for me to realize that he was speaking on the telephone. And by that time I knew who he was speaking to.

"No. It seems to be someone totally unconnected with her mother and Marissa. Some man."

He was listening now to whatever Susan Shrink was saying, and I waited.

"God, no! I never thought of that." Pause. "I think she'd have told me if she thought he was a messenger sent from her mother. I'm sure she would."

My heart was pushing itself against my ribs. A messenger from my mother? How could they ever . . .

Dad was talking again.

"Not good. She's got that balanced-on-the-edge sound to her again. I should never have taken her away. She was doing better there, with you."

I imagined him, leaning his head against the wall the way I had done, maybe tracing the same riverlike crack with his finger. "I know I mustn't panic." He listened some more. "She shows no interest whatsoever. I'm beginning to believe she means it." That would be my dancing. Between them they were covering a lot of ground.

"Wait a second," Dad said. "I have a pencil right here. What was that name again? Dr. Rinehart, 2840 Van Ness. Do you have his phone?"

I began backing away, but I could still hear.

"It's unforgivable calling you at this time of night. It must be almost one there. I'm just so terrified that she's going off again . . ."

I turned and ran back up the stairs.

I should have known what would happen, and in a way I had known. But I hadn't been able to see another way out. Now there was going to be a new doctor.

Maybe Dad would take us away from the Rookwood house. But he didn't think this—this thing—had anything to do with living here. He thought the sickness was inside of me, and that if we moved I'd take it with me. I was on my own then.

For a minute I thought about running away, and in the same minute I thought about JoJo.

"You won't leave the way Mom and Marissa did, will you, Cinnamon-Pie? Not ever, ever?"

"No, JoJo. Not ever, ever."

I'd left once, of course, when they'd taken me to the hospital. But I'd had no choice then. I wouldn't go now. Felix Ferrero was not going to drive me over the edge. I would fight.

I got out of bed again and opened my door. Downstairs I could see the slit of light under the kitchen door. Dad was still in there, probably thinking over what Susan Shrink had said. Probably planning how he could get me to this new doctor without making me suspicious.

I edged into the bathroom. There was no need to put on the light. I knew exactly where I'd put those letters, and I stood on the lid of the toilet, leaned over and slid my hand under the Rookwood sheets and towels to the back of the cupboard. I touched the corner of the small pile, and this time a jolt shot up my arm. It was the kind of jolt you get when you bang your elbow, and your arm goes numb from the wrist up. It hurt so much I felt weak.

I took a shaky breath, forced my hand to close over the envelopes and pull them out.

Chapter 11

When I wakened in the morning I lay very quietly, looking at the letters on my bedside table. I stretched out a hand and touched them, and they quivered like a frightened animal.

Today I would see Lisa.

Dad and JoJo were eating cereal at the kitchen table. Dad wore his usual tweed jacket. I wondered if Dr. Rinehart's phone number was tucked in the top pocket. "My daughter, Cinnamon. I'd like to have you see her. Dr. Abbot recommended you."

The classified section of the Chronicle lay by his bowl. Well, he was going to try to get me away from here anyway. That was something. There were penciled circles here and there on the open page.

"Any possibilities?" I asked.

Dad looked at JoJo and shook his head. Of course. There was no point in getting JoJo steamed up about this till we had to. He wouldn't want to leave Donna just when he'd found her. Already I felt like a rat.

"How are you feeling this morning, Cinnamon?" Dad asked.

"Better." What would he think if he knew I'd lain, reading ghost letters, till almost morning?

"Today I hid in the avocado grove and watched them cut down our tree," he'd written. "I knew it was doomed from the night he caught you. And then I saw a man putting bars on your bedroom window. Oh, Emily! What is your father doing? Does he mean to keep you prisoner till he takes you away from me altogether?"

Love letters, with enough joy and pain in them to make me cry.

I sat at the table and then stood up again. "What's the weather like? Is it foggy?"

I walked casually through the living room to the big window. It didn't matter to me if there was rain or sun. But I had to know about Felix. Was he there already? Maybe he never went away.

The car waited in the driveway behind Dad's Honda, and now I could see all of it, the way I'd been able to see all of him yesterday. It was black, square-angled and sharp-cornered. The hood was yards long and it had a cloth top. A step thing at the side held a spare wheel. Five big headlights glittered in the sun, two up high and three below. It was a car that belonged in a museum behind a velvet rope. His precious *Cord*.

"I'll be there at midnight. The Cord will be in the usual place. Be careful coming down, and for heaven's sake, make sure both your parents are asleep."

The Cord. How old was it now? Like Felix, it would be this age forever.

He lounged behind the wheel. It was too far for me to see his face but close enough to know there was a face. I stepped quickly back.

"So what are the plans for today, Cinnamon?" Dad asked as I took milk from the refrigerator.

"Not much. I'm going to walk into Sausalito and prowl around." That was true. I'd get the bus to the city from there.

"I thought I might take the day off and follow up on some of these." Dad's fingers touched the *Houses for Rent* he'd marked, and he smiled his fake casual smile while his eyes slid away from mine.

"Follow up on what?" JoJo picked up his cereal bowl and drank his dregs of milk.

"Don't do that, JoJo." I pulled out a chair and sat. Dad not going to work? Impossible. He didn't even take the day off when we arrived. But I *wanted* him to go today. I had plans.

I spread butter on cold toast. "Couldn't you call from the office? Or maybe I could do it? Yeah. I'll make a list of the possibilities and phone them all this afternoon."

JoJo banged his spoon on the table. "You guys! What possibilities? Nobody tells me anything."

"What are *you* doing today, JoJo?" Dad asked.

"Going to Donna's. Painting some more." JoJo leapt from his chair. "I gotta go now. She said come early."

"Are you sure it's okay with her mother?" I asked. What a blessing *that* would be, to be free of JoJo while I went into San Francisco.

"I told you. She likes me. She likes me just as much as she likes Donna."

113

Dad laughed, and I sensed his relief too. For a minute I didn't understand. Then I did. I bent my head over my plate, cutting my toast into smaller and smaller pieces. Dad didn't want his little son left with a freaked-out sister. That's why he was going to stay home. Now he could relax. So what was he going to do in the future? Hire a competent baby sitter? For a second I truly hated him.

He got up and stretched. "Well, if you've both got things going maybe I'll just head for the office then after all." He took a twenty dollar bill from his wallet and set it beside me. "You might need some spending money, Cinnamon. Why don't you treat yourself to lunch?"

I didn't even say thanks.

He was struggling to say something else and at last he got it out. Talk about the ultimate in fake casual. "You didn't have any more bad dreams, sweetie? No ghosties or ghoulies or things that went bump in the night?"

I shook my head. This was the way he was going to handle it then. Felix had been just a bad dream that I'd told him about, a bad dream that we could both forget. Okay, Dad. It was a mistake to tell you. So now let's both pretend that it never happened.

JoJo and I walked him to the front door and waited while he got into the Honda. Felix waited, too, sitting straighter behind the wheel. I wouldn't let myself look at him directly. I waited then while JoJo ran across to Paul's house.

The motor of the Cord started with a roar, and I retreated. He was moving up to the spot just below the

114

porch steps where Dad had been parked. I ran inside, closed the front door and leaned against it.

The San Francisco map almost covered the kitchen table when I spread it out. Immediately I saw that the ferry would be the best way to get close to Mission. The street began about a block from where the boat docked. Once there, the Computer College wouldn't be that hard to find.

I got dressed quickly.

Presumably Felix knew I was here alone. But presumably he didn't know I was going to see Lisa. I hadn't been able to get away from him before. But was that because I'd always gone out by the front door where he waited and could follow me? That was a possibility and the only one I had. I didn't want him with me today. So I'd take a different route.

I was half way down the stairs when the doorbell rang, turning me rigid. Felix? Who else could it be? Did he think I'd open it for him? And did he need it opened to come in?

I tiptoed down the rest of the stairs and saw JoJo's face pressed against the living room window. His fingers tap-tapped on the glass.

I opened the door.

"Faddle, Cinnamon! How come you keep this locked all the time?" he asked indignantly. "When I go out, I can't get in again."

"What happened to staying at Donna's?"

"She got a call for an audition." JoJo struggled between disappointment and pride. "That means a try-out for a commercial. Her agent called her. That's a man who handles all her jobs."

"Oh. I see."

"So she had to go, and her mom had to take her, and I couldn't go, too, because they don't allow friends. Even best friends."

I decided quickly that I wasn't going to put off seeing Lisa and that I'd have to take JoJo with me.

"Listen, JoJo. I'm riding the ferry into San Francisco this morning. Want to come?"

"The ferry? Jumpin' jiminy. For sure I want to come!"

"Who taught you to say 'for sure'?" I asked, seeing Paul's face laughing down at me. "You're going to have to say 'for sure, Cinnamon,' like a good Californian."

"Oh, Donna says that all the time."

I folded the map. "Was Paul there, or has he gone to work?" Boy, I was almost as good as Dad at fake casual.

"Naw. He was there. Are we going on the ferry right now, Cinnamon?"

"Right now. Get a jacket." I paused. "What was he doing?"

"Who?"

"Paul."

"Nothing. I'll go get my jacket."

I wondered how come JoJo talked all the time, but when I wanted to know something I couldn't pry it out of him.

While he ran upstairs I checked to see if Felix was still there. The big black car sat, silent as a hearse, by the front steps. Felix stood, his back to me, polishing it. He bent down to run a cloth over the low, sleek fenders. I saw that his pants were a light cream color, too wide for today's fashions. His shirt was a shade darker. "The guy was a flash dresser," Paul had said, looking at the photograph that day in the rose room. For sure. The whole scene was like something from *The Great Gatsby*. A time for playing, for long, lazy days on the river. But Felix wasn't there and neither was the car and I hadn't seen a river since I left Massachusetts.

JoJo came pounding down the stairs.

"Donna's not wearing her flippers today 'cause she has to say *marshmallows* and she says it real funny with her flippers in. Paul says the way she says *marshmallows* with her flippers in is so disgusting it could put you off them for life. She was going to lend them to me for the day but her mom wouldn't let her."

"Too bad," I said automatically, noticing how my heart jumped at the mention of Paul's name. Weird.

JoJo was heading for the front door. "Come on, then, Cinnamon."

I grabbed his arm. "Listen, I thought we'd try going down through the garden and out at the bottom by the little house. Sort of explore."

"Okay. Donna says the best apples in the whole world are in that garden but you have to go through stickers and prickers and stuff to get to them. Donna says its okay to take them, for the Rookwoods just let them rot."

I could tell it was going to be a day of "Donna says." Donna says "take three steps" and we all take three steps. Donna says "jump" and we all jump.

Very quietly I opened the door that led from the kitchen to the side of the house.

"Now," I whispered. "Let's go."

"Why are we whispering?"

"It makes it seem more of an adventure."

JoJo beamed. "For sure."

We went stealthily down through the long, dry grass. There were rocks here, big as footballs, and clumps of weeds with heavy, yellow blossoms. There was poison ivy. I guided us carefully around it. A tumbledown shelter or gazebo lay at the bottom of the first dip and there was a rusted wrought-iron bench. I looked back. From here I couldn't see the driveway. But the car had still to be there. No traffic had gone by on the street since we started.

We were at Mrs. Cram's fence now. I found a small gate and we edged through. No smoke came from her chimney, and all her windows were still draped tight. A neighbor must have been taking care of her garden, though, for the earth in the flowerbeds was dark and damp, and a green hose coiled across the path. We went out on Anderson Street, safe and hidden from the Rookwood house by the dip in the road.

"Hey, Cinnamon, that was fun. Should we still whisper?"

"No. We can talk normally now."

We crossed Bridgeway on the corner by the market where we'd bumped into Paul, and then passed Sonny's Pizza Place where he worked. It wasn't open yet. *Oh Paul. I've only been here a few days and everything and everywhere reminds me of you!*

For the first time we walked on the wide sidewalk that ran into Sausalito by the side of the bay. It was a heavenly morning with water blue and sparkling. Only a trace of fog hung in a shimmery veil between us and

San Francisco across the bay. A loaded barge glided silently under the bridge. One of the white and blue ferry boats was part way across, coming this way. With any luck we'd be on it for the return trip.

It was all so beautiful. I could have loved it here, walking along with Marissa. I imagined how "up" she would have been.

"Oh, look, Cinnamon. Look at that rock! It's shaped just like a darling seal. Let's go sit on it."

"Marissa! They'll think we're idiots."

"Oh, who cares? Come on, Cinnamon-Stick!"

I swallowed. If Marissa and Mom were still alive we wouldn't even be here. But I miss you so much, Marissa. If only I could turn the days back.

A solitary sailboat headed straight for the horizon and I thought of the Pied Piper. "You want peace?" he'd asked. I did, but I wasn't going to get it. He wasn't either.

We passed a lady with a little girl and I stopped them to find out where the ferry came in. The lady told me to keep heading the way we were going, that I couldn't miss it. There was a park with stone lions, and the ferry docked just behind it.

We found the park and the lions, and the ferry was just nosing in. I used Dad's twenty to buy our tickets, and in a few minutes we were aboard and moving.

As we pulled away from the dock I could see the houses of Sausalito climbing the sides of the narrow, winding roads to the wooded hills behind. I could see Anderson Street and our house, dark and brooding at the very top. Its glass glittered in the morning sun, signalling to me. I made myself look away.

From here Sausalito was beautiful, all little beaches and flowering vines and wharves where sailboats lay. It seemed an enchanted place. And maybe it was.

"Are we going to stop at Alcatraz?" JoJo asked excitedly.

"I hope not." Alcatraz was not exactly what I needed right now, but I leaned across the railing with all the other passengers as we sailed by, close enough, as JoJo said, to spit. I stopped him from trying.

We came into the dock at San Francisco just as the clock on top of the ferry building chimed once for ten thirty.

There was a delicatessen outside the turnstile and I bought JoJo two doughnuts, one for now and one for later. The way I remembered it, we should go left. To be certain, I asked a man in a raincoat where Mission Street was, and he told me it was just a couple of blocks away.

JoJo looked up at me as we walked. His face was powdered with sugar from nose to chin. "How come we've come over here, Cinnamon? Is it to do with the ballet school?" Little, tentative hopeful voice. I thought what I'd thought plenty of times before. JoJo is pretty smart for such a dumb little kid.

I started to shake my head and stopped. Ballet school would certainly be a good reason if Dad found out where we'd been. And there was no way he wouldn't, with JoJo along. He'd hear every bit of it, from beginning to end.

"Maybe I'll check out that ballet school," I said. "I'm not sure."

JoJo smiled up at me. "You used to like it a lot."

"I know."

We were walking past numbered piers. Joggers panted by. Men and women walked their dogs. Between the concrete square buildings I could see blue wedges of bay and the span of one of the bridges—I'd no idea which one. On the other side of the boulevard the city streets seemed to start, disappearing into the tall skyscrapers. There was Mission. I grabbed JoJo's arm. "We'll cross here."

The Computer College turned out to be only about a hundred yards from the start of the street. If I hadn't been looking, we could have walked right past it. It was a house like all the others with glass doors in front and the college name etched on them. A man and a girl sat on the low red brick wall that bordered the sidewalk.

"Excuse me," I said. "Do either of you know Lisa Berringer?"

They looked at me and then at each other and shook their heads.

"Is there an office where I could ask?"

"Sure. But it's almost break time. Chances are she'll come out in a few minutes with everybody else to grab a smoke or a breath of air."

"Oh, fine. I'll just wait then."

I guided JoJo to a spot farther along the wall.

"Is this the ballet school?" he asked.

"No."

"Who is this person, Lisa? She's not the Loony Lisa one that Donna knows?"

"This one is not loony."

"Do you know her from home?"

"No. She's from Minnesota."

"Oh." It's amazing how easy it is to satisfy JoJo

121

sometimes. If I answer exactly what he asks and volunteer nothing, he loses interest fast.

The man and the girl had been right about break time. Suddenly the sidewalk and the little flagstone area in front of the glass doors twittered with students. I heard snatches of unintelligible conversation.

"I kept feeding the data in, and it wouldn't swallow it."

"Maybe you've got the wrong variable."

A guy stood by himself, drinking Tab from the can.

"Excuse me. Do you know Lisa Berringer?"

He tilted his head toward the doors. "That's Lisa over there. Striped sweater."

I looked and saw her. She had a round, Little Orphan Annie face and big Orphan Annie glasses. Her hair was a blond fuzz that made her head twice its normal size. Somebody thirty pounds heavier would have fitted her jeans and striped sweater without any trouble. I watched her lean against the wall by the doors and light a cigarette.

"JoJo, will you sit right here for five minutes and eat your other doughnut while I talk to her?"

"You won't go away?"

"I promise. You'll be able to see me all the time."

"Okay."

I pushed my way through the crowd. "Hi," I said. Her smile was friendly. "Hi."

"I'm Cinnamon from the Rookwood House. Sausalito? I called you."

She was taking a drag on the cigarette, and the smoke went the wrong way. She choked and tears fogged up the round glasses. I waited while she recovered. She snubbed the cigarette out against the wall, took off her glasses, wiped her eyes with the back of her hand and put her glasses back on.

"I need to talk to you," I said.

"No."

"Please." I touched her arm. "I'm truly desperate. I promise, if you'll just talk to me for a few minutes and help me understand what's going on, I won't bug you anymore."

She took off her glasses again. There were two sharp, red marks, one on either side of her nose, and she massaged them. Her eyebrows were narrow penciled lines.

"It's about Felix," I said. "I can't handle what he's doing, and a first I thought I was going cuckoo again, like I was before, but now I don't think so; I think he's really here and . . ." Geez! I was crying, and I'd been talking so loudly that the groups closest to us were all staring.

JoJo came running across. "Cinnamon? Cinnamon, what's wrong?" In a second he'd be crying too.

"Ssh," I said. "It's all right."

Lisa was looking at me, blinking like a little blind mole. "I don't even want to remember," she said at last. It was the light, childlike voice I knew from the phone call. "God, but you're as desperate as I was." She put her glasses back on. "Okay. Let's go somewhere."

I sniffed and held onto JoJo's little, warm, sticky hand, and the two of us followed her back the way we had come. There was a small outdoor cafe with round tables and metal chairs. It had potted geraniums and a view of the bay. A guy with his back to the railing played guitar with an open guitar case waiting hopefully at his feet.

"This all right?" Lisa asked and I nodded. If I'd tried to speak, I think I'd have blubbered again. We sat and Lisa ordered coffee for us and an ice cream cone for JoJo. It came first.

"You don't need to sit with us," I told him shakily. I fished fifty cents from my purse. "Here. Why don't you go over and ask the guy to play something for us."

JoJo slid down from his seat.

"Poor little kid," I said. "Doughnuts and ice cream. He'll probably have a stomachache tonight and that'll be my fault too."

"Your little brother?"

I nodded.

"No sisters?"

"No," I said.

Lisa rolled her eyes. "You're lucky."

The coffee came and I leaned across the table. "Lisa. Tell me about Felix. You saw him, too, didn't you?"

Lisa began blink-blinking again. She took her glasses off and rubbed the two red marks between finger and thumb. I thought she wasn't going to answer, and then she said, "I was just like you. Sometimes I thought he was there, and sometimes I was sure I was dreaming him."

JoJo waved at us frantically as the theme from Star Wars drifted toward us.

I nodded and smiled. "Good, JoJo."

Lisa stared into her coffee cup. "Are you using?"

"Using? You mean drugs? No way!"

She looked up. "I was, you see. Everything. My father brought me here to get me away from bad influences while my good sister, Beatrice, was sent to summer camp." She smiled her Little Orphan Annie smile. "You can't *ever* take a kid away from bad influences. She'll find new ones. It didn't take long. I just went on the beach. Hung around the parking lot at the movie house. My poor father! I was freaking out all the time." She shook her head. "I tried to tell him about Felix. But Felix went right along with the headless horse that used to chase me and the giant cucumber. Have you ever been eaten by a giant Pac Man cucumber? So he got me away from there fast."

I leaned toward her. "Tell me about Felix."

"He's dead. He's a ghost. He's a hungry ghost. That's what they call his kind that wander the earth, searching for something or someone. I know. I did plenty of ghost reading—then and since."

"But what does he want from me? Why can you and I see him and nobody else?" I didn't mention the Pied Piper. He was another story.

"I can't tell you that for sure! He came slowly to me. It took a while before I really saw him."

I shivered. "I know."

JoJo came running back, and I gave him another fifty cents. "What should I get?"

"How about 'Rudolph the Red-Nosed Reindeer,'" Lisa suggested.

"But it's not Christmas."

"He won't care. You'll see," I told him.

"It's Emily he's looking for, of course," Lisa said

when JoJo left. "You know about Emily who slept in the room with the arched window? God, that was the all-time creepiest room."

I nodded.

"He killed her, you see," Lisa said. "And he's dying of guilt." She gave a little laugh. "Dying . . . get it? He wants to tell her how sorry he is, but he can't find her on the other side. He thinks they loved each other so much that she must be searching for him, too, and that one of these days he'll find her and she'll forgive him for what he did."

"He killed her?" My heart was pounding. "How do you know all this stuff?"

"He told me. Just wait for it. He'll be talking to you too, pretty soon."

I leaped up, jostling the table so the coffee spilled.

"Sit down," Lisa said quietly. "You wanted to see me. I'm here. But I'm leaving in five minutes and that's it."

I sat, trying to get my thoughts in order, wishing I'd made a list of what I needed to ask her. I remembered my theory about why Felix was haunting me.

"Lisa? Did *you* ever kill anyone?"

The thin eyebrows lifted and she blinked frantically at me though her glasses. "Kill? Are you crazy? Of course I never killed anyone." She looked down into her coffee cup. "There was for a while . . ." she stopped.

"What?" I prompted. "Please tell me. It's . . . it's crucial."

"Well, my dear sister, Beatrice, tried to hang it on me that I was responsible for my mother's stroke. She

126

died, just before that summer. Of course, most of the time I was too spaced out to know *what* Beatrice was saying. But not really. I suffered. God, how I suffered. So what did I do? Heavier on the pills, that's all. A doctor I talked to helped straighten me out. He said that embolism that killed my mother was probably floating free in her bloodstream for umpteen years. It took its own time to lodge in one of those important places." Lisa swallowed. "After a while I was able to visualize it, you know. It helped."

I put my hand over hers that lay on the table. There wasn't anything I could say. When your mother dies, there just isn't much *to* say.

She sucked in a deep breath. "In case you care, I'm okay now. It took a lot of time and a lot of pain, but I'm clean."

"Earlier you said you didn't know for sure why Felix comes to us. Did you ever try to guess?"

She nodded. "And he said something to me once. I asked him, 'Why me?' or something like that. Why didn't he go to someone who'd known Emily, and he said, 'Everyone won't let me in.' " Lisa shrugged. "I just figured he needed to use a doper, like me."

I shook my head. "It's not that."

I was half watching JoJo. Someone had joined him in front of the guitar player. I recognized that back instantly. The pale cream slacks, the shirt that was just a shade darker, the cap perched on the black, curly hair. I pushed my knuckles against my lips. Of course he'd found me. He always did.

"Lisa?" I whispered. "He's here. Felix."

"Where?"

I nodded toward the guitar player. "Beside JoJo."

Lisa turned. I saw her head move left and right. "Where? I don't see him."

"You don't?"

"No," Lisa said softly. "There's only JoJo and the guy making the music. You mean he's here, but he's not here for me." She pressed her hands together and closed her eyes. "I'm okay, then. I'm finally okay. I always figured I wouldn't be as long as I could see somebody who isn't really here and . . ." She stopped. "Oh, Cinnamon. I'm sorry. I don't mean . . ."

If she had said anything else, I didn't hear it because for the first time I was looking directly into the eyes of Felix Ferrero.

Chapter 12

JoJo and I took the one o'clock ferry back. Clouds had gathered, black in the sky, and the bay was dark and choppy. Few passengers braved the upper deck, and those that did, huddled with their coat collars turned up against the wind.

I was cold as death.

"I don't feel so good, Cinnamon," JoJo moaned as the boat bumped and smashed into the waves. Poor little JoJo. A stomach full of garbage and then this.

I didn't feel so good myself. I'd hoped for comfort from Lisa, but there hadn't been any. All there had been were more things to scare me and make me wonder about myself.

Where was Felix now? Riding the ferry with us? Transferring himself in some strange ghost way through time and space so that he'd be waiting again in front of the Rookwood house?

I remembered his face and shuddered. Not a death's head, as I'd imagined. Not a skeleton. But so terrifying it had made me step backward, bumping into my chair, sending my purse skittering across the ground. *I* was haunted, but no more than he was. It was there in his eyes. I'd never seen such eyes . . . hollow, hungry. That's what Lisa had called him . . . a hungry ghost. No human being could know such misery and live. But he wasn't a human anymore and he wasn't alive either.

I turned my face into the wind and pulled my jacket close around me. A shimmer of rain had driven everyone but JoJo and me below. There were only the two of us, and a seagull perched on the flagpole at the stern.

"I'm going to be sick, Cinnamon," JoJo said, and I held onto the back of his jacket as he leaned over the railing and was.

"Good thing there was nobody back there," he said as he finished and wiped his mouth on the Kleenex I gave him. "Did you see the way it all blew back? Did you see that seagull take off?"

"I saw."

Some adventure this had been. Some fun trip.

We went back along Bridgeway and straight up Anderson Street. No need to detour through Mrs. Cram's and the Rookwood gardens. There was no fooling Felix. He knew our every move.

Dad's car was in the driveway and I checked my watch. Two forty. How come he was home so early?

He met us at the door.

"Where *were* you? I decided to come back after lunch to check if everything was . . ." He stopped. "To do some phoning. And I went across for JoJo, and he wasn't there." A muscle in his cheek jumped and twitched. I looked at it instead of into his eyes.

"Mrs. Russell and Donna had to go out unexpectedly. I took JoJo with me."

"I know that. She was back and she told me. But where *were* you? It's almost three."

"They're back?" JoJo said. "Whoopeee!"

"You told me to treat myself to lunch," I said.

I knew why he'd come home, all right. It had nothing to do with phoning. He'd been frightened about me. I thought about that, and I tried to find love and comfort in it. But there was a sneaking underlying feeling that pushed itself to the top. He'd wanted to make sure JoJo was still all right and safe from his crazy big sister. I should understand and not blame Dad too much. But that was hard for me right now. I needed support and belief from someone other than a stranger like Lisa.

Dad made an effort to smile and be hearty. He clapped JoJo on the shoulder. "So what did you do all day, big fellow? Have a good time?"

"I had ice cream and doughnuts and then I threw up. I got a seagull right in the eye. Wait till I tell Donna. Can I go?" JoJo was poised, ready to run.

"Just a minute," Dad said. "I don't know if Mrs. Russell's going to want you this afternoon. We're all invited over there for dinner. Seems it's Donna's father's birthday."

"For dinner? Great." JoJo paused for five seconds. "But she'll want me. She's probably just waiting for me to come so me and Donna can help her. Yeah, maybe to make the cake." He stopped again. "Is Donna going to be the marshmallow girl?"

"I didn't ask."

JoJo rolled his eyes.

131

"All right. So go," Dad said.

I took off my jacket and slung it on the couch. We were going to Paul's for dinner tonight. Would he be there? Surely he wouldn't miss his own Dad's birthday. He'd reschedule his work, or do whatever he had to do. I'd made another discovery. It wasn't necessary for me to hear Paul's name for that little thrill to hit me. The thought of seeing him was enough to start the tingling. What would we say to each other?

"So where did you go today then?" Dad asked.

"Into San Francisco. We took the ferry."

"Oh. If I'd known you were planning on going to the city, I'd have given you a ride this morning." Dad could switch to his fake casual as easily as a car on automatic could switch gears. But I heard the little change in his voice and stiffened. "Any particular reason you went?"

Not to register in ballet school, if that's what you're hoping, I thought. Not to see Dr. Rinehart, whose existence I'm not supposed to even know about.

I shrugged. "I thought it might be fun to ride the ferry. That's all."

"Oh." I could even spot a fake casual *oh*. Something else was coming.

"By the way, I just happened to be passing that ballet school, the one I told you about? And it was like fate . . . there was a parking spot right in front so I popped in and picked up one of their brochures. You might like to have a look at it. I put it on the table by your bed."

I nodded. "Thanks." He'd have been racking his brains. Then he'd remember that ballet school. Poor

132

Dad! Ten points for trying. The brochure would be on the table next to Felix's letters.

"He's looking for Emily, of course," Lisa had said. "He killed her, you see."

Killed her. Killed her. Killed her.

"Are you all right, Cinnamon?"

I'd have to face it. From here on in Dad would be watching me very carefully, maybe even keeping notes for Dr. Rinehart the way I'd always suspected he kept them for Susan Shrink. At least mentally.

"I'm fine. It's just what I told you. I hate this house. I hated coming back to it today. Can we start calling the places in the paper?"

"Sure." He touched my hair, smoothing it back with a gentle hand. "We'll find something, honey. I promise."

I swallowed. Sometimes he could be so wonderful and so understanding. I'd thought about that a lot. He was understanding when it was something he had no trouble understanding. Not everything to do with me fitted that category any more. He just couldn't believe me, that was the trouble.

By five o'clock we'd called all the numbers Dad had marked. When we said we wanted to rent for only the summer we weren't too popular, and it seemed nobody liked kids. We kept on telling them how good and well behaved JoJo was. Once Dad's voice got really mean and he said, "Yes, but not when he gets excited!" He slammed the receiver so hard on the hook that it almost pulled the phone from the wall.

"Honestly! She asked if JoJo was housetrained."

I put the cup of coffee I'd made on the table in front

of him, and we grinned at each other. I felt close to him again. My own Dad. He really did love us and he was pretty much all I had left.

"Let's not get a wall phone when we have our own place," he said. "There just isn't the same satisfaction slamming the receiver when it's hanging from a hook."

In the end we were left with only one possibility. It was a condominium in Corte Madera.

"Where is that?" I asked.

"If you get the map, I'll show you." Dad didn't say anything when I took the map from my purse and spread it on the table. Corte Madera wasn't very far from Sausalito. I didn't know if that was good or bad. If we moved there, I might still be able to see Paul—if he wanted to see me. But was it far enough for me to get away from Felix? Would he follow me if I lived in another house, or did he stay here, wanting a physical presence in the house that had once held Emily, needing hands that touched where Emily's had touched?

"Just one possibility in all that bunch," Dad said, shaking his head. "That's not so great. We'd better move fast on it too. I'd say we'd go tonight except for the Russell's party, so we'll plan on tomorrow night. I'll call and make an appointment."

"Fine. What time do we go tonight?"

"Six o'clock, she said."

"I'd better go then and have my shower."

Standing under the hot water, I tried to think. What I needed was a common denominator. Felix had killed Emily. The Pied Piper, Lisa and I had all been responsible for deaths. Whatever Lisa said about inevitable embolisms, I knew she had to feel she'd played a big part in what had happened to her mother.

"I suffered. God, how I suffered," she'd said. Me too. So, someone had died because of us. If there was another common denominator, I couldn't find it. Except that we were all loony and that I wouldn't accept. But why couldn't she see Felix now? What had changed? Wait! There was something she'd said— some key. I almost had it but it slipped away.

I dried off carefully and allowed myself to think about tonight. What had Paul felt when his mom told him we were coming? Was he glad? Did he still want to see me in spite of . . .?

I smoothed after-shower lotion into my skin. It smelled of flowers, but not roses. Gardenias maybe. My hands lingered on the smooth curves of my thigh and stomach. The long mirror was steamed, so I saw myself as through a mist. The tangle of dark, damp hair hanging on my shoulders, the smooth long curve of waist and legs.

Unthinkingly I reached for the towel rail and held it the way I'd held the barre in the studio, arching my back, flexing my legs. "You're going to be a very great dancer some day, *chérie*." I seemed to hear Colette's voice and then my mother's, filled with love and confidence.

"Of course, you must stay. But Marissa and I'll stay too. I can't bear to miss seeing you."

"Mother! Then I'll really feel guilty about spoiling your trip too."

I stared into the misted mirror. What was that? I leaped for a towel, then relaxed. It was only Dad's old robe, hanging on the back of the door, and not Felix behind me.

There'd been something in one of those letters.

"You will have to come to me, Emily. Since your father put me out, I will never set foot inside that house again. But my heart will be there with you."

Old-fashioned words. Thinking about it, I knew I had never seen Felix physically inside the Rookwood house. He must have kept his word. But he projected his mind in and his power. It was probably safe to stand here and look at myself in the mirror, though, and wonder if Paul would like what I saw. *Oh, come on, Cinnamon, cut it out. He's never going to see you like this, and thinking about this kind of stuff will really drive you crazy!*

I wrapped the towel tightly around me and padded back to the bedroom. What should I wear? A birthday party sounded dressed up, but who knew? I decided on my white pants and my one and only silk shirt. The pants look like linen, and the shirt is a pale pink with a V neck, low-cut but not obscene. The sun and wind had made my cheeks and nose pink too. I decided I looked almost healthy. Almost normal.

I used the curling iron on the ends of my hair to tame it a bit, and at the last minute I put on my yellow cap, the one Paul had bought for me on Fisherman's Wharf.

"You look pretty nice," JoJo told me as I came down the stairs. "Clean. That's because you used every bit of the hot water, you pig." He tried to grab my cap, but I stepped back. "What's with the cap? That part looks dumb."

"Never mind," I said, and Dad added, "I think it's great. She's telling everyone she likes San Francisco."

Didn't he just wish!

He had found two bottles of wine somewhere to bring and we locked the house and left.

The Cord sat in the driveway with Felix at the wheel.

"He'll be talking to you pretty soon, you know," Lisa had said. My heart jumped. Awful. Awful.

I stopped at the bottom of the front steps looking down at the round flower bed filled with weeds that lay directly under the arched window. A golden dandelion head bent to the touch of my sandal.

"There was once a tree here," I said, and I leaned back to look up. "It went all the way to that window."

JoJo took my hand. "Is this a fairy tale? Rumplestiltskin or something? Was there a princess?"

"Sort of."

"How do you know about the tree, Cinnamon?" Dad asked.

"Someone told me."

He put his arm around my shoulder, and I felt the wine bottle, cold against my cheek.

"Let's go, people," he said and Felix turned to watch as we walked across the street. I had no doubt he'd be joining us.

It was strange walking up the driveway to Paul's house. This was where he lived, and that made it special. Maybe he cut the grass, though it didn't look as though it had been cut for a while. Which was the window of his room?

Mrs. Russell met us at the door.

"Welcome." She smiled at me. "You look lovely, Cinnamon, and I do like your cap! It's too bad Paul had to work tonight. But we have invited the Donaldsons from down the block, and they have two teenagers, so you won't be totally bored. Jim's sixteen, I think, and Susan's younger."

I tried to smile back. Paul wasn't going to be here! The hair curling, the silk shirt, the whole thing for nothing! I'd been using my imagination. I'd been dreaming he'd say, "That's the cap I bought for you, isn't it?" And he'd look down with those wonderful eyes and say "Pretty!" the way he'd said it then, and everything would be all right between us again. It wasn't going to be that way. And I bet he could have gotten off. He'd probably thought, "Crazy old Cinnamon's coming, so I'll just pass."

Several people were gathered in the Russell's big, beamed living room. We met Paul's dad and wished him happy birthday. He was tall and gangly with nice eyes with laugh lines around them. But they weren't golden like Paul's. Maybe there weren't any other eyes in the whole world like Paul's.

We had dinner outside, and everyone was nice. The Russells had a glassed-in deck with a view of the bay, warm behind glass walls. Below, the bay seemed hung with Christmas lights, and we could see San Francisco gleaming like a bright picture etched on dark glass. I wanted to cry.

There was barbecued chicken and fresh corn and birthday cake. Afterwards Mr. Russell turned on the stereo in the living room, and music floated through the open windows onto the deck.

"All Sinatra," Mrs. Russell said. "He loves Sinatra."

Mr. Russell danced with his wife, and I saw the way he laid his cheek against her hair. I wanted to cry again. Dad was leaning back in his chair, watching them too. He had that faraway look on his face. Was he thinking of Mom? I blinked away tears.

Boy, Cinnamon, I told myself, *you're a real plus at a party*.

JoJo and Donna bunny-hopped around, hands joined, stopping every now and then to kick up their legs, shout "Marshmallow!" and giggle in some sort of secret ritual.

I danced with Dad and Mr. Russell and with Jim Donaldson twice, and I tried to talk and laugh and act as if I were having a good time. Normal, I told myself. Normal girl at a party.

And then I heard Donna shout "Paul!" and I saw her gallop across the deck to the living room door and there he was. Paul!

"Hi, everyone," he said, and my heart was doing all that funny stuff again. "Happy birthday, Dad," he said. "I got here as quickly as old Bozo would let me off."

"Great. There's still some cake," his mom told him.

I guess Jim Donaldson and I went on dancing. I listened to what he was saying, but my mind was concentrated on Paul. He disappeared inside the house, maybe to have his cake, and then came back out. I thought he'd combed his hair. He stood sideways to me, talking to Mr. Donaldson, so all I could see of him was the side of his face, the smooth, brown curve of his throat and the long, thin length of him. Once he laughed and I melted.

He danced with the Donaldson girl.

He danced with his mother.

He danced with Donna.

I smiled a lot and tossed my hair and settled the cap at a more rakish angle. He never came near me.

The moon was shining now, reflecting on the bay,

gleaming pale through the skylights on the deck. One of the ferries cruised silently across the dark water, lights glittering from stem to stern. I swallowed down the horrible lump in my throat and moved across to the glassed-in railing.

"So how's it going, Cinnamon?" It was Paul beside me, his words so ordinary and horrible, the kind you'd speak to just anyone.

"Okay, I guess," I said, not even turning my head in his direction.

We stood in silence, and that space that had been between us when we walked on the beach was still there, wider than ever.

"How's Felix?" he asked suddenly.

My heart slithered. "Who?"

"You know, the guy you're really talking to when you tell me to bug off and leave you alone."

I didn't answer. What was there to say? But I turned briefly to look at Paul and saw Felix too. He lay in one of the lounge chairs, his eyes closed.

"Once, when I was a kid I knew a guy called Sammy Voss," Paul said. "He had an imaginary friend that he used to play with all the time. His friend's name was Tobe. Tobe and Sammy played ball and everything. No matter how hard we tried, none of the rest of us could see Tobe, and I used to envy the heck out of Sammy. I mean, it was pretty nice for him, having Tobe around all the time." He stopped. "Is Felix your imaginary friend, Cinnamon?"

"Something like that."

I saw a smile flicker briefly across Felix's face.

"What if I asked you to dance, then, and you said 'no.' If you said, 'I never want to see you again

140

because you were pretty rotten to me in the car,'
should I just figure you're talking to Felix again and
you're not mad at me at all?''

Behind him, Felix stood and stretched.

"I—I—" I began.

Felix was walking toward us.

I turned quickly back to look sightlessly down on
the bay. *Stay calm, Cinnamon. Don't mention that
he's there. Don't speak to him. Be careful. Careful.*

"Will you dance with me, Cinnamon?" Paul's voice
was unsure. On the record Sinatra was singing,
"Strangers in the night, exchanging glances," and
Paul's shoulder was touching mine, his hand so close
on the railing that if I moved just an inch . . .

"Cinnamon?" Felix said.

Oh, no. All my blood seemed to have oozed out,
leaving me here, emptied. I held onto the railing.
"He's going to talk to you pretty soon, Cinnamon,"
Lisa had said. "Pretty soon." Oh, no.

"I . . . Paul . . . could you get me a glass of
lemonade? I'm . . . really thirsty."

"Sure. Are you okay?"

Careful. Be careful, Cinnamon. Normal.

Somehow I squeezed out a smile. "Must be the
effect you have on me."

"Hmm. Dehydration? I don't know if that's good or
not. I'll be back in a minute."

"Will you help me find Emily?" Felix asked.

I waited till Paul was halfway across the floor, but
still I whispered. "I can't. Why me? I never even
heard of Emily till . . ."

Paul was filling a glass now from the lemonade
pitcher on the table.

141

"You can help," Felix said. "You can talk and ask people. I can't get to everyone. I don't know where she's buried. I think they took her away. Alive and dead they took her from me." Rough voice. Hoarse. An accent of some kind.

Paul was coming back.

"I'm not asking anyone anything," I said quickly. "I'm not talking to you. I'm leaving here, and it's your fault. You're really selfish, you know. Just because you and Emily are dead, you don't care about anyone else. Me or Lisa or anyone . . ."

His hands were touching me, ghost hands. The ghost eyes, filled with misery looked into mine. "Please help me. I have to find her. You'll never see me again."

"Let go of me," I whispered fiercely, but he didn't, and I knew what was going to happen.

"Emily liked to dance," he said, and the ghost hands were strong, pulling me toward him, moving me so that I had to move too or be dragged. And we were dancing in some unreal nightmare dance across the floor where Dad was and Mrs. Donaldson and all of them. I saw the faces, amused, puzzled.

" 'Chevalier' was Emily's favorite," Felix said and I knew that I wasn't even here for him, that in his memory it was Emily he held.

Paul had stopped halfway across the floor. I couldn't bear to look at him.

It was Donna who yelled, "Hey! Look at Cinnamon. She's dancing all by herself. What are you doing, Cinnamon. You look funny!"

Her little, ridiculing voice gave me the extra strength I needed to break free of Felix and run.

Chapter 13

I ran across the dark street. I ran up the steps to the porch of the Rookwood house, flung myself against the front door, but it was locked and Dad had the key. I crouched down then, cowering against the wall. "Please," I whispered. "Please."

There were voices now coming in my direction. I heard Dad calling back to someone. "She'll be fine. She's easily upset these days. No, truly. Thanks anyway, but I think it will be all right."

What must they have thought, all those people? Dancing by myself, my arms stuck up in the air, talking to an invisible person? But had I talked? I couldn't remember. I'd tried so hard to be careful. Please don't let me have talked.

I saw them then, Dad and JoJo and a couple of other people hovering behind . . . all of them except Dad and my little brother turning reluctantly back to the Russell house.

"Cinnamon?" Dad called softly. "There you are, honey."

I sensed his relief.

And JoJo. "What did you run for, Cinnamon? You're such a baby. Just cause we teased you." And then, hesitantly . . . "What's the matter, Cinnamon-Pie?"

I stood and Dad put his arms around me. "Ssh," he said.

I held on to him as if he were an anchor. "It was . . ." I stopped. I'd been going to say, "It was Felix again. He was there, dancing with me." But what point was there in that? One craziness was only worse than another. "It was the music," I finished. "And, remembering." That was partly true.

Dad patted my back. "Let me just get the door open here. You can slip right into bed. Can I do anything for you?"

"Nothing. I just want to go to sleep."

JoJo tugged at my shirt. "Lots of people dance by themselves, Cinnamon. I've seen it on TV. Even you used to. When you danced the Sugarplum Fairy, remember . . ."

I hugged him tight. "That's true, JoJo."

The scent of roses was overpowering as I ran up the stairs and it seemed to me I could see the perfume lying pink and humid in the air, flowing in to hover over me as I lay rigid in bed.

The phone rang, and Dad came tiptoeing into my room. I tightened my grip on my mother's hairbrush and pretended sleep. He tiptoed out again. Maybe it was Paul. But what could I say to Paul either?

Later I heard JoJo come upstairs and then Dad. The

old house was suffocating me, pressing in on me. I had to get away from it and from *him*. But did the two go together?

"Will you help me find Emily?" he'd asked. "You'll never see me again." All right, Felix. You win. I'll help.

I sat up in bed and switched on the lamp. The ballet brochure was on the table, a purple dancer on a silver cover. AUGUST 31–JUNE 12, it read. I turned it face-down on the table. On the back was a registration form, and I picked it up again and read automatically:

All new students with at least a year of ballet training who wish to enter the Professional Division must audition for acceptability and class placement. Auditions will be held Sunday, August 9, in the San Francisco Opera House Ballet Studio.

It was hard not to feel something. I could imagine the studio: the bare wooden floor, the barre on three sides, the wall-to-wall mirror on the fourth. Drab, empty, filled only with those smells of sweat and powder and dust. I felt the tears come, but this wasn't the time for tears. There was a blank white shiny area below the registration form and I found a pencil and began a list.

1. Check the newspaper files.
2. Check the death records.

I switched off the light then and lay down. Susan Shrink had been right about one thing. Lists helped, even short ones. They got the muddle out of your head and onto the paper. But there was a vacuum where the muddle had been, and through it, I felt again Felix's ghost hands, his ghost body touching mine.

I guess I drifted off into an uneasy sleep, the smell of roses still around me. When I woke I knew it was very early, not long after dawn. The light had that woeful gray look to it. Somewhere a dog howled. Jasper, maybe, up in the hills. Someone else's life that Felix had managed to mess up. And for the first time I remembered telling him how selfish he was. A hungry, selfish ghost.

I padded to the bathroom. JoJo's door was open, his porthole window a circle of half light. I went across to it. Early mist clung to the weeds in the slope of garden outside and drifted around the ruins of the old gazebo. The bay was flat and a dull pewter color. I was about to turn away when I saw something else. A thin trail of smoke rose from Mrs. Cram's chimney. She was back! I remembered my list of last night and my heart quickened. If I'd known Mrs. Cram was home, I'd have put her name first.

"She's lived here for ever and ever," Paul had said. She'd be sure to know something.

I ran back to my room and checked my watch. Five thirty. Did the fire mean she was awake or only that she kept it burning day and night?

I found my jeans and sneakers and pulled on my sweater as I ran down the stairs and out of the back door.

The tousled garden was night wet. I slipped and slithered, heading for the gate JoJo and I had used yesterday. If there were no sounds from inside, I'd sit

146

by the fence and wait, but if there were, I'd knock and plunge right in. She'd think me crazy. Five thirty in the morning! But everyone else thought I'd flipped, so she might as well join the crowd.

There was no doubt that she was awake.

Jazz music came from the cottage and I heard a woman's voice saying: "Down, down, stretch, stretch. All the way to the floor now." There were small thumps and grunts from inside.

I knocked but nothing happened except that the same voice commanded, "Stretch it out. Stretch it out." A television voice, and too wide awake for this time of morning.

I knocked harder and the door jerked open.

I was looking down at a tiny person, no bigger than JoJo. She wore black leotards with blue leg warmers and her silver hair was piled in a tidy, elegant chignon on the top of her head.

"Yes?" she asked. I'd never seen so many wrinkles on a face and I'd never seen such skin, soft as crumpled silk.

Behind her was a living room about the size of a closet. It was jammed with stuff that it couldn't begin to hold. Things were piled on things, but tidily. There was the sense of order you'd find on a small boat. A fire glowed in the tiny hearth. A circular rug, patterned in red and yellow alternating rings lay in the middle of the clutter and in front of it was a TV set switched to an exercise program. The girl on the screen stood bent over, looking at me backwards from her spread apart legs. "Stretch," she called. "Stretch." Her bulging blue eyes laughed up at me.

"Yes?" Mrs. Cram asked again.

"I . . . ah . . . I hope I'm not disturbing you. I'm Cinnamon. We're living in the Rookwood house."

"Come in." She stepped aside and closed the door behind me. "Will you have a seat while I finish with Debbie?"

"Thanks." I sat.

"I work with Deb every morning, and a nice girl she is too. It's a fine way to start the day," Mrs. Cram said.

"It must be."

I sat silently in awe, as the two of them cavorted and leaped, twisted and impossibly turned to the beat of modern jazz. When the cooling down exercises began and Mrs. Cram sat on the rug, limp and lolling, I knew we were almost at an end. She asked me to wait then while she had a shower.

"I won't be five minutes, love. Will you have a bite of breakfast with me? I'm sorry to keep you sitting here, but neither one of us could stand me without my shower. I smell as bad as an old dog my father used to have when it came in out of the rain."

"Take your time."

I looked around the room. There was a model of a sailing clipper in a glass bell jar on top of a bookcase. A ship's clock hung on the wall and there were lots of photographs. One was of a seafaring gentleman in uniform. He must be Mr. Cram. There were several of the same woman at various ages. That was probably their daughter. I saw one of Emily in a pale, floating dress. Maybe the one that had been in the trunk. She smiled at the camera, and I recognized her instantly.

When Mrs. Cram came back she had changed into nice fitting jeans with a pretty pale blue shirt tucked neatly into the waistband. The silver chignon was held in place by a filigree silver comb. She put a kettle to boil on a gas stove that must have been as old as she was.

We had grapefruit juice and warm blueberry muffins for breakfast. I'd watched her take the muffins from a round red tin box with a picture of a castle on the lid.

"My passion," she said as she buttered her second. "It's part of the reason I need Debbie."

I sipped at the tea that was so strong and bitter it made my eyes water. "Are you English, Mrs. Cram?"

"English? Bite your tongue, girl! I'm Irish. From County Clare. But that was a long way back before I met my darling husband, the finest man that ever walked the earth." She pushed aside her plate and poured another cup of tea from the pot.

"What brings you down so early, lovey? I'm enjoying it, mind. But I'm thinking there's more to it than you've let on."

I crumbled the last bite of muffin on my plate.

"I want you to tell me about Emily and Felix," I said. While I'd sat waiting for her to shower, I'd decided how much I should say and how much I should leave out. Honesty about Felix didn't pay. I'd discovered that already. "I know a little about them from the stuff in the house," I said. "There are trunks."

"Emily's things are still there? After all this time?"

"Stored," I said. "In a room the Rookwoods don't seem to use."

"Aye, well. It was all left in a hurry, and I suppose nobody bothered to disturb it. They might think the McWhirters would want it, sooner or later."

149

"Can you . . . tell me about them? I'm curious."

"Curious? Aye, you would be, seeing her things." She put her elbows on the table and her chin in her hands. "Emily McWhirter and Felix Ferrero!" Her face took on a remembering dreamy look. "That was a sad story all right. I'm thinking there aren't many sadder."

"She lived in the Rookwood house?" I prompted.

"She did. Only it was the McWhirter house then. Her daddy built it, and a grand place it was, sitting up there, lording it over the rest of us below. Oh, they had the best of everything. The finest furniture. Even a grand piano, though not a one of them could play."

She took another muffin and buttered it absently.

"They were old money, the McWhirters, and in those days that was everything. Always in the society columns. Jenny McWhirter, that was Emily's mother, had no health at all to speak of, and there were always doctors coming and going. He brought them from Chicago and New York . . . every place. It was like a miracle to them when they had Emily. Neither of them was young any more, you see. That was part of the trouble. He was like an old rooster with a new young chick."

I waited while she took a bite of muffin and poured herself more tea.

"A spot more to heat yours, darlin'?"

"Thanks. I'll pass."

"Aye, there was nothing good enough for Emily. Oh, what a dour man he was, Robert John McWhirter. Scotch Presbyterian stock than which there's none dourer. But he loved Emily. Loved her with a passion.

They thought for a while of sending her away to a private school, for there was nothing around here he thought splendid enough for his daughter. But they couldn't bear to let her out of their sight when it came right down to it. And he was one of the pillars of Sausalito, you see. It wasn't much more than a fishing village in those days, but it had promise."

"So they sent her to school here?" I asked.

"Yes. And it was in the high school that she met Felix. She came down here and told me about him, right from the first. What a pretty thing she was, with her long, dark hair and that pink and white complexion." She looked at the photograph. "That's Emily in her graduation dress."

"Yes," I said.

"The good Lord only knows where she got her looks, for it wasn't from *him* or *her* either. She always smelled of roses. Not a heavy, sickly smell, but gentle, you know. Like flowers in the morning. Her father got the soap for her all the way from Paris, France. Not even ordinary soap was good enough for Emily." Mrs. Cram shivered and looked down at her hands. "I've never been able to abide the smell of roses since. I can't have them around me."

"She fell in love with Felix?"

"She did. Like a ton of bricks. And no wonder either. He was like a film star, poor Felix, and very dashing. His people had money too and, oh, the way he dressed, fancy as a lord. And his car! I don't recall the kind now, but it was the most talked about car in all the country, and him no more than a boy. But that's the way *his* father was, as proud as Robert John

151

McWhirter and hoping always he could buy his boy's way into society. It didn't work then. I don't know if it does even now."

She found a blueberry on her plate and popped it in her mouth. "They were Portuguese, you see. Started from nothing. Felix's father had been a fisherman with a head for business. He opened his own fish markets and they did well. He had one here and a couple in the city. None of that changed things a bit in Emily's father's eyes. Felix was nothing."

"But they . . . Felix and Emily . . . they got together anyway?"

"Oh, aye. It wasn't easy for Emily to defy her parents. They met on the sly. Emily slept in that room with the arched window that's right over the driveway. There was a tree, and she'd come down at night and Felix would be waiting in his car. I don't believe there was any hanky-panky, mind you. Just hand holding and a kiss or two and maybe a bit of touching here and there."

The thought of Paul came to me, his lips against my hair, his hands . . . I thought I knew how Emily felt. Those things didn't change.

"Oh, they were mad for each other." Mrs. Cram's voice was soft.

Yes, I thought, and Felix can't even stand glass in that window now. He won't allow it.

Mrs. Cram was talking again. "To see them together was a treat. You never saw such joy in two of God's creatures in all of your life."

I remembered the photograph I'd found. Joy was the right word.

"Her father put a stop to that. He found out what

152

she was doing, and he cut down that tree and even put bars on the window. 'That'll end it, my girl. Shaming us like this.' That's what he said to her. She came down here, weeping like a baby, and storming and ranting too, for she had a temper. Oh, aye, she was raging. But what could she do? Robert John sent a car with a driver to pick her up every day after school, and they kept her near a prisoner. And all the time they were making arrangements for her to be going to some highfalutin school in Boston.''

I smiled a little, thinking of my highfalutin school in Boston! Pot smoking in the bathrooms. Beer behind the gym. Robert John McWhirter wouldn't have approved of it at all.

"So she did all she could do. She and Felix ran away."

I sat forward. "Where did they go?"

"Not far, lovey. Not very far. They came here to say good-bye to me the day before they left. It was all planned."

I saw the unshed tears in her eyes. "There was a thing about Felix that I haven't told you. I never saw a sign of it myself, mind, and Emily never believed it, not then. But there was talk. And after what happened . . ."

"Saw what?" I asked. "Talk of what?"

"Well, who knows what drove him to it. Maybe the heartsickness over Emily. Maybe the insults he got in this town from people who thought the Ferreros all had ideas above their station." Her fingers played absently with the sugar bowl. "Felix took to drink. He'd be all right for a while and then he'd go on a tear and he'd be away from school, sick, you know, and there were people who saw him, staggering around, falling down even into the gutter. And him only eighteen years of age."

"But couldn't Emily stop him?"

"You don't stop a drunk, lovey. Not if he wants to keep on drinking. And they never discussed it, for she told me that. He never said anything to her, and if he had, she wouldn't have believed it. To her he was perfect, and anything anybody said against him was a lie out of jealousy. Nothing more. Well . . . he was drunk that night. The night they ran away."

Her head was bent over her teacup so I could only see the top of the shining knot of hair. "The car was going all over the road. It nearly hit Joe Van der Veer on his way up the hill, and there were plenty of others that saw it. It never made it round the bend there onto Bridgeway. Down the hills it went, swerving from side to side, and Emily with her suitcase beside them and Felix with that everlasting cap on his head. It hit the cliff on the corner there, and then it bounced and skidded and went over the sea wall. It's not much of a drop, only a few feet to the beach, but whatever happened it went up like a torch. We could all see the flames, though we didn't know what it was or who was in it, burning down there. The McWhirters stood up above me on their deck, thinking their Emily was safe behind her bars. I don't know to this day how she managed to get out of the house to go with him that night. It was bad cess that she did."

We sat in silence. When she spoke again, Mrs. Cram's voice was soft. "Ah, I had the death guilt for a while all right. You know what the death guilt is, Cinnamon? When you think you were the cause of somebody's going on before his time? And I had it. After all, I knew what they were planning, and maybe I could have stopped them. The two of them wouldn't leave my head. And there was one time I even thought I saw Felix, standing right there by that door, and that pitiful looking."

The death guilt! I could scarcely breathe. That was it, of course. The common denominator. *I* had it. The Pied Piper had it. Lisa had it and got over it, and Felix . . . Felix had been destroying himself with it since the day he and Emily died. Our guilt let him in. Mrs. Cram was still talking, but I was having trouble hearing, my mind so abuzz now with my own thoughts. Lisa had stopped feeling guilty and Felix had gone. That's what I'd almost understood yesterday. I started to listen to Mrs. Cram again. "Then he held out his hands and he said, 'Where's Emily, Nellie? I can't find Emily. They've taken her again.' I tell you child, I near died of fright. I took myself off to my daughter's for a while, and we talked and I got over my nonsense. 'People make their own decisions, Ma,' my daughter said. 'Do you think you could have stopped them? Guilt is only self-pity anyway, and you never were one for that, Ma.' " Mrs. Cram smiled wanly. "I can't stand self-pity, and Mary Margaret knows it. Besides, I don't have enough life left to go wasting it, now do I?"

Who does? I thought. You think at *my* age I have time left to waste? But how do you turn guilt off? There isn't an on/off switch. Maybe you try to be reasonable and say, "People make their own decisions. Do you think you could have stopped them?" Could I have stopped Mom and Marissa? Probably not.

"Where was I? Oh, yes. Seeing Felix. Well, thanks be to heaven, I never laid eyes upon him but the once."

My tennis shoes were cold and wet, and the bottoms of my jeans stuck to my legs. I shivered. He'd given up on Mrs. Cram, too, the same as on Lisa. I'd learned so much this morning. I'd maybe even learned some things about myself. But there was still that question that I had to ask. For Felix. And for me.

"Where . . . where did they take Emily to bury her?"

Mrs. Cram's eyes opened wide. "Bury? Bless you, child. They didn't bury her anywhere. Emily isn't dead."

Chapter 14

Emily's not dead?" I sat, stunned. Not dead?

"She was thrown from the car. Many's the time I've thought about seat belts, and how if we'd had them then she'd likely have been trapped inside. But she was burned terrible, all the same. They took her to Ross Hospital first, and then to a private plastic surgeon in New York."

I couldn't believe it. Not much wonder Felix couldn't find her in that other existence.

"He thinks he killed her," I said. "All these years . . ."

"What? What do you mean, child?"

"I . . . he probably thought he killed her . . . just at the second when it happened."

"I doubt if he had time to think, and his head befuddled anyway with the drink."

"Is Emily still alive? Now?"

"Oh, bless you, yes. She's only a young woman, not

much past sixty. She's back in Sausalito, living in a townhouse on Rodeo Drive, one floor up with a nice view of the bay. I visit her often, but she never comes here. Too many memories, I suppose, and who can blame her? She's gone a wee bit queer, you know. And who can blame her for that either? She's away a lot on trips, studying sea life. She always was a great one for the sea life. I don't know if she's home now or not."

I stood. I was shivering all over, and I hugged my arms tight around me. "I have to go, Mrs. Cram. Thanks for breakfast."

"Darlin', you don't look so good. I shouldn't have kept you talking like this, and it such a sorrowful story."

"No," I said. "I needed to know. But now I have to go."

I went back up Anderson Street. I'd have to change, and find where Rodeo Drive was and get money for the bus. What would I say to Emily if she was home and I found her?

Felix sat on the ledge that ran like a wide step round his car. He jumped up when he saw me coming.

"Like a film star," Mrs. Cram had said. Yes. But a worn one, who'd been around too long. An old man, playing the part of a boy, with old eyes that had known too much pain.

"You were with Nellie Cram," he said, and it wasn't a question.

"Yes." I edged around him. My skin felt clammy.

"She let me in just once. Then she stopped me."

"I know."

Old, gravelly voice. Had it always been like that?

The accent . . . Portuguese. Mr. McWhirter had probably had a Scottish burr. But he would have thought that different.

"Does she know where I can find Emily? Does she? Does she?" His hands lifted toward me and I stepped back.

"She—she—" What if Emily wasn't back yet from that trip? What if . . .

He strode forward and grabbed my wrists. I saw the mole, small and golden, in the hollow of his throat.

"You're hurting me," I said, but he didn't loosen his grip. His breath was old on my face. I turned my head away.

"Emily thought I was drunk that night. As if I'd ever risk her precious life. But she didn't know." The fingers were so tight that I felt my hands going numb. "I'll tell *you* what was wrong with me, Cinnamon Cameron. I'll tell you, and I never told her. I had epilepsy. All my life I had it, though my father never believed it."

"But . . ."

"Don't ask me why I didn't tell her. Can't you see why? It was bad enough being who I was. And an epileptic too? It wasn't hard to keep it a secret. Most of the time I was normal. I could go months without an attack and I always got a warning. I had time to pull over if I was in the car. There'd be colors, lights behind my eyes. That night there was no warning."

He let go of my wrists and put his hands over his face so I could hardly hear him. "You know what her last words were? 'How could you do this to me, Felix? How could you get drunk, tonight?' And then she

159

screamed, and then I lost her in the flames." He shuddered. "All these years . . . knowing what she thought. That I killed her senselessly, needlessly . . ."

I rubbed at my wrists and began backing away. The death guilt! The wedge that he used to push through to the rest of us. What a waste of a life it was. What a waste of a death.

"That's why she doesn't come to me, you know," he said. "She's wandering alone, as I'm alone. If I could find her, find where they laid her, I could tell her. I could . . ."

I wanted to shriek, "She isn't dead." But I was afraid of him and afraid of what he might say or do. Instead I took one step away, then another, running round the side of the house, reaching the safety of the back door. Inside, I stood panting, pushing my fist against the place in my chest where my heart pounded.

"He took the drink," Mrs. Cram had said. And Emily had asked, "How could you get drunk tonight?" But he hadn't.

I ran quietly into the hallway. There was no sound from upstairs where Dad and JoJo probably still slept.

A square, white envelope had been pushed under the front door. I picked it up and saw my name on it, and I knew the writing, though I'd never seen it. The note inside was written on a piece of ruled notebook paper.

Dear Cinnamon,

I don't know what's wrong, but something is. Whatever it is, I'll help you. There'll be two of us then to face it together. Okay? I tried to call tonight, but you were asleep. Tomorrow I don't go to work till noon. Will you call me and we'll talk.

Paul

P.S. About Alison. She's a friend—a good friend. That's all. I wanted you to know.

I held the note against my cheek before I put it back in the envelope. It was as sweet and wonderful as anything Felix had ever written to Emily. It didn't have *Love* at the end, but I knew. *Do you mean it that Alison's just a friend? I think you do. Oh, Paul! When I come back from Emily's, one way or the other, I'm going to tell you everything. Felix says if I help him find her he'll leave me alone. I'm going to start working on my senseless guilt too. I've promised myself that. But shutting it off so he can't get to me will take time. I don't have that time.*

I changed and looked up Emily's phone number, but it wasn't in the book. Maybe it was better this way. I left a note for Dad, telling him I had to go out early and unexpectedly, and that he shouldn't worry, though I knew he would. There was no way to explain. Then I slipped Paul's letter into my pocket and left. It was ten minutes past seven.

Felix sat in his car. I went across and spoke through the open window. "You asked me to help you, and I'm going to try. There are some things I want to check out . . . newspaper files, death notices. I'll tell you what I find, but please don't come after me. You make me so nervous I can't think. I'll be back in a little while."

The deep eyes examined me, looking for truth, and

seemed satisfied. In a way it was true. If I couldn't find Emily there'd be nothing else for me to do.

"All right," he said. "Thank you."

I hurried down the hill.

When I got to the junction of Anderson and Bridgeway where the car had hit on that night so many years ago, I slowed. But if the crash had left a mark it had eroded away, or else it had been covered by the big, white, square graffiti that crawled over the cliff. I glanced down at the beach, too, picturing the Cord burning and Felix burning, picturing them both now, up at the McWhirter house where it had all started.

I rode the bus through the shimmery summer morning, with early sun glinting off the water, turning the bay from gray to a clear bottle green. A girl with flyaway hair and long, skinny legs skated on the sidewalk in front of the shops. She could have been Marissa except that Marissa was gone. And I had to let her go. But I would always remember.

We lumbered past yacht moorings where boats lay, reflecting themselves in the still, clear surface. Cormorants sunned themselves on a distant rock. Early fishermen cast off from the wooden docks, their lines splintering the water.

The bus brakes squeaked. "Rodeo Drive," the driver called, his eyes meeting mine in the rearview mirror.

I got off and crossed the highway.

Far up in the sky a purple kite streamed out, catching the high breeze. A red poster on a telegraph pole advertised a circus and fireworks on August 9. August 9. There was something about that date that was important for me, but right now I couldn't remember what.

Rodeo Drive ran into the hills, too, the apartment buildings all new and all clones of each other with walls of glass and small, wrought-iron balconies.

I didn't know which one Emily lived in. But I knew it had to be in the front because Mrs. Cram had talked about a view of the bay. I found it easily. The mailbox said McWHIRTER, #14, and I walked up the outside concrete steps that angled to the front door. A mobile of seals cut from black shells dangled by my hand as I rang the bell. *Be here, Emily. Be here. But if you are, what will I do? What will I say?*

The door opened.

It was Emily. I wanted to run.

"You're back," I said stupidly.

"Yes. Who are you?"

"We're renting your old house . . . on Anderson Street. Mrs. Cram told me where to find you. I need to talk with you."

"Come in."

I sat in a wicker chair with a peacock back, and she sat on a flowered couch facing the window and me. Sunlight fell cruelly on her face. The mouth that had smiled in the two photographs had a hard tightness to it. Creases ran from the corners of her lips to her nose. If the plastic surgery had left scars, they were hidden among the other lines on her face. Her hair was still long, more gray than brown now, and pulled back into a barrette. But the changes I saw were not from the passing of years. Something else had done this, made her mean-looking, angry. Maybe that was what pain did. Or sadness. Behind her on the wall was a wooden plaque with different kinds of whales etched on it. A smooth gray walrus made from stone was the only thing on the coffee table. The whole apartment was bare and impersonal, like a motel room where someone was stopping for the night and then moving on.

"Do you want my permission to get rid of the stuff?" she asked.

"The stuff?" What was she talking about?

"What's left of all that junk," she said impatiently. "In the old house. Is it in your way?"

"Oh. Oh, no. It's fine. Everything's in the one room. It . . . doesn't bother us." And that was as close to a downright lie as it was possible to come. But I did need a reason for being here. "It's . . . about the music box," I said. "It's so pretty and it's just lying in one of those old trunks. Would you mind if I . . ."

"Take it. Take anything. I told Georgie Rookwood years ago to pitch all that stuff out. I'd never come for it. I guess she didn't do it."

"Pitch it out?" I couldn't believe she'd said that. The picture of the two of them. The letters. The yearbook. My dark and lovely valentine. "You must want *some* of it," I said hesitantly.

"You know about Felix, don't you?" She had a way of speaking that was strange to me, as if she bit off every word.

I nodded.

"Did Nellie tell you that too?"

"Yes. I hope you don't mind." I ran my hands along the rough, rattan arms of the chair.

"Felix Ferrero." The name was a curse the way she said it. "What a crazy fool I was. I should have listened to my parents. But at least they had the satisfaction of knowing they were right in the end. My mother died three years ago, and my father six months after that. It gave them great pleasure every day of their lives to remind me of my narrow escape from Felix."

I swallowed. This woman was filled with hate. Hate was what had hardened her and turned her eyes to stone.

She stood and walked to the window, her stride too fast and furious for the small room. Her pleated, tartan skirt swirled angrily. "Six years," she said. "Eleven surgeries. Taking a piece off me here and sticking it on there."

I started to say, "You look very well," but I was scared to speak. This was a scary person. I moved to the edge of the chair. In one second I'd stand and I'd say, "Well, nice to meet you and thanks for the music box," and I'd split. "She's at Fourteen Rodeo Drive," I'd tell Felix. "But Felix, she isn't dead." The rest would be up to him. I wished him luck. "I've done my part," I'd tell him. "Now you leave me alone." If he did, we might not have to go from the McWhirter house. But I knew already, I'd still want to.

Emily swung around to face me. "He was falling down drunk, you know. Did Nellie tell you that? Eyes rolled up in his head, couldn't sit straight. Slobbering. Did she tell you I was trying to lift him off me, that he'd fallen over when the car hit the cliff?"

"Stop!" I stood too. My legs were shaking, and so was my voice. "That's not fair. He had epilepsy. Do you think he'd risk your life by getting drunk? You were everything to him." Oh, no. Why was I defending him like this? Now she'd ask me how I knew, and what would I say? But she just stood, staring at me, the color gone from her face.

"Epilepsy? But how . . . What do you know about Felix? Tell me!" She grabbed my wrists the way Felix had done and her hands were strong and hurting.

"I found . . . proof. In the house. It's true."

Her eyes looked deep into mine. I saw something shifting in them, like colors changing on the surface of the sea. "She's gone a bit queer, you know," Mrs. Cram had said. Little specks darted in those eyes, fish swimming up from unknown depths. I began to think the hands and the eyes would never free me.

At last she stepped back. "I believe you. What you're saying is the truth. But why did he never tell *me?*"

"I guess he thought he'd lose you. Back then, people were ashamed of illnesses like that. It was a bunch of crock, but they were." It was dumb talking to her about "back then." She'd been there back then. But she wasn't listening to me anyway. She sank onto a footstool, her elbows on her raised knees.

"Epilepsy?" It seemed hard for her to get past the word and the thought. "Yes. That time . . ." She was talking to herself, not to me. Remembering. "We went to Muir Beach. And he got so strange looking. And he left. He was gone for ages. I was cross with him."

I stood, uncomfortably, wishing my words unsaid. What did all this matter now?

She jumped up and paced again. She slumped back on the footstool. Her face was bloodless. "I didn't smell liquor that night. The police asked me. But there could have been reasons for that." She stopped. "If

I'd known, I might have been able to help him. He didn't trust me enough and that must have been my fault. I think I always condescended to him. I mean, I was my father's daughter after all. And he died . . . Felix died . . . Felix, my love . . ." Her voice rose to an almost wail.

I was scared, but I was sorry for her, too. "You couldn't help it. He didn't tell *anybody*." I stretched out a hand to touch her shoulder and her head tilted to look up at me.

"Oh, my God, what did I do to him? All these years . . . hating him. Blaming him. Oh, Felix!" She stiffened and looked at the door. I looked, too, though I'd heard nothing and I saw nothing either. But she did.

Sometimes in a house at night, a dog will raise its head and gaze intently into space. Its nostrils flare. It may growl deep in its throat knowing something that no one else knows. That was how Emily was. She sat straight. She stood.

She smiled.

I felt my heart begin its slow steady thumping because I knew who was there and why. The death guilt. After all these years Emily had it, and now Felix could get to *her*.

"Don't, Emily," I said desperately. "Don't blame yourself. It's only self-pity, and if you do Felix will come and he'll take you . . ."

It was too late. She walked slowly toward the door. "Felix," she whispered.

I blinked. Her back was toward me, and I couldn't understand when or how it had happened without my seeing, but now she was wearing the tiered cotton skirt and the white blouse. I saw the anklets and the white saddle shoes that were in the trunk, back in the rose room of the McWhirter house.

Someone took her hands and whirled her round and round and she was laughing, her face filled with joy, the barrette gone from the dark hair that swung free around her.

"Felix? Are you there?" I whispered. No one answered because there was no one there for me. He'd let me go as he'd said he would. He'd never be there for me again. I circled around them.

Emily was speaking. "Of course I will, Felix. Don't I always go with you when you ask?"

And then I was outside, running down the shadowed concrete steps, her words pounding in my ears, the scent of roses all around me. She was going with him . . . where? I slowed. I shouldn't have told her.

"Cinnamon," I said out loud. "Are you going to feel guilty about this now? For Emily's new happiness? For Felix, finding what he's searched for all these years? For bringing them back together? You're not, Cinnamon," I said. "She has a choice and it's her choice. She's free to make it."

Outside the sun shone golden and warm. A city bus was cruising in my direction, heading for the Sausalito center. I ran and I got to the stop in time to catch it. My hand closed over Paul's letter in my pocket. He didn't go to work till noon. He'd still be there.

I got off the bus on Bridgeway and I walked up the three hills, hurrying, hurrying. Someone sat on the wall of the McWhirter house. It was Paul. The night I'd first seen him he'd vaulted across that wall and into our driveway. "I never do things the easy way," he'd said. Well, I didn't either.

He sat now, swinging his legs, the sun finding the red in his thick, brown hair. "Hi," he said.

"Hi." I took a deep breath. "It's all over, Paul."

Paul slid from the wall and put his arms around me. "Oh, I don't think so," he said, smiling down at me. "The bad things may be over. But the good things are just beginning."

About the Author

Eve Bunting was born and went to school in Ireland. She moved to California in 1958.

Ms. Bunting began writing in 1969 and has written more than a hundred books for children and young adults. Many of her books have won awards. She writes every day, usually in the morning, and says, "I consider a day wasted when I don't write."

Ms. Bunting once lived in a house in Sausalito that was the inspiration for the setting of *Ghost Behind Me*. While she lived there, she never observed any ghosts. However, while she was working on the novel, she decided to visit her former house. She discovered that the house really is haunted and has been listed in the National Register of Haunted Houses!

Ms. Bunting and her husband now live in Pasadena, California. They have three grown children.